KINGFISHER • TREASURIES

Ideal for reading aloud with younger children, or for more experienced readers to enjoy independently, Kingfisher *Treasuries* provide the very best writing for children. Carefully chosen by expert compilers, the content of each book is varied and wide-ranging. There are modern stories and traditional folk tales and fables, stories from a variety of cultures around the world and writing from exciting contemporary authors.

Popular with both children and their parents, books in the *Treasury* series provide a useful introduction to new authors, and encourage children to extend their reading.

KINGFISHER
An imprint of Larousse plc
Elsley House, 24-30 Great Titchfield Street
London W1P 7AD

First published in hardback by Kingfisher 1988
First published in paperback by Kingfisher 1991
8 10 12 14 16 18 20 19 17 15 13 11 9

A CIP catalogue record for this book
is available from the British Library

ISBN 0 86272 807 X

Printed and bound in Great Britain

A · TREASURY · OF STORIES · FOR
SIX
YEAR OLDS

CHOSEN BY
Edward and Nancy Blishen

ILLUSTRATED BY
Tizzie Knowles

Kingfisher

CONTENTS

GIACCO
AND HIS BEAN
Florence Botsford

Once upon a time there was a little boy named Giacco who had no father or mother. The only food he had was a cup of beans. Each day he ate a bean until finally there was only one left. So he put this bean into his pocket and walked until night. He saw a little house under a mulberry tree. Giacco knocked at the door. An old man came out and asked what he wanted.

"I have no father or mother," said Giacco. "And I have no food except this one bean."

"Poor boy," said the kind old man. He gave Giacco four mulberries to eat and let him sleep by the fire. During the night the bean rolled out of Giacco's pocket and the cat ate it up. When Giacco awoke, he cried, "Kind old man, your cat has eaten my bean. What shall I do?"

"You may take the cat," said the kind old man. "I do not want to keep such a wicked animal."

So Giacco took the cat and walked all day, until he came to a little house under a walnut tree. He knocked at the door. An old man came out and asked what he wanted.

"I have no father or mother," said Giacco. "And I have only this cat that ate the bean."

"*Too* bad," said the kind old man. He gave Giacco three walnuts to eat and let him sleep in the dog kennel. During

the night the dog ate up the cat, and when Giacco awoke, he cried, "Kind old man, your dog has eaten my cat!"

"You may take the dog," said the kind old man. "I do not want to keep such a mean brute."

So Giacco took the dog, and walked all day until he came to a little house under a fig tree. He knocked at the door. An old man came out and asked what he wanted.

"I have no father or mother," said Giacco. "I have only this dog that ate the cat that ate the bean."

"How very sad!" said the kind old man, and gave Giacco two figs to eat, and let him sleep in the pigsty.

That night, the pig ate up the dog, and when Giacco awoke he cried, "Kind old man, your pig has eaten up my dog!"

"You may take the pig," said the kind old man. "I do not care to keep such a disgusting creature."

So Giacco took the pig and walked all day until he came to a little house under a chestnut tree. He knocked at the door. An old man came out and asked what he wanted.

"I have no father or mother and only this pig that ate the dog that ate the cat that ate the bean," said Giacco.

"How pitiful!" said the kind old man, and gave Giacco one chestnut to eat, and let him sleep in the stable. During the night the horse ate up the pig, and when Giacco awoke he cried, "Kind old man, your horse has eaten up my pig!"

"You may take the horse," said the kind old man. "I do not want to keep such a worthless beast." So Giacco rode away on the horse.

He rode all day until he came to a castle. He knocked at the gate and a voice cried, "Who is there?"

"It is Giacco. I have no father or mother and I have only this horse that ate the pig that ate the dog that ate the cat that ate the bean."

"Ha! Ha! Ha!" laughed the soldier. "I will tell the King."

"Ha! Ha! Ho! Ho!" laughed the King. "Whoever heard of a bean that ate the cat that ate the dog that ate the pig that ate the horse!"

"Excuse me, Your Majesty, it is just the other way around," said Giacco. "It was the horse that ate the pig that ate the dog that ate the cat that ate the bean."

"Ha! Ha! Ho! Ho!" laughed the King. "My mistake! Of course, it was the bean that ate the horse; no, I mean the horse that ate the bean; no, I mean – Ha! Ha! Ho! Ho!" laughed the King, and the knights began to laugh, and the ladies began to laugh, and the maids began to laugh, and the cooks began to laugh, and the bells began to ring, and the birds began to sing, and all the people in the kingdom laughed and sang, and the King came to the gate and said:

"Giacco, if you will tell me every day about the bean that ate the horse; I mean the horse that ate the bean; no, I mean the horse that ate the pig that ate the dog that ate the cat that ate the bean – Ha! Ha! Ha! Ha! Ho! Ho! Ho! Ho! – you shall sit on the throne beside me."

So Giacco put on a golden crown and sat upon the throne, and every day he told about the horse that ate the pig that ate the dog that ate the cat that ate the bean, and everybody laughed and sang and lived happily ever after.

THE FLYING POSTMAN
V.H. Drummond

Mr Musgrove was a Postman in a village called Pagnum Moss.

Mr and Mrs Musgrove lived in a house called Fuchsia Cottage. It was called Fuchsia Cottage because it had a fuchsia hedge around it. In the front garden they kept a cow called Nina, and in the back garden they grew strawberries . . . nothing else but strawberries.

Now Mr Musgrove was no ordinary Postman; for instead of walking or trundling about on a bicycle, he flew around in a Helicopter. And instead of pushing letters in through letter-boxes, he tossed them into people's windows, singing as he did so: "Wake up! Wake up! For morning is here!"

Thus people were able to read their letters quietly in bed without littering them untidily over the breakfast table.

Sometimes, to amuse the children, Mr Musgrove tied a radio set to the tail of the Helicopter, and flew about in time to the music. He had a special kind of Helicopter that was able to loop the loop and even fly UPSIDE DOWN!

But one day the Postmaster-General and the Postal Authorities sent for Mr Musgrove and said, "It is forbidden to do stunts in the sky. You must keep the Helicopter only for delivering letters and parcels, not for playing about!"

Mr Musgrove felt crestfallen.

After that Mr Musgrove put his Helicopter away when

he had finished work, till one day some of the children came to him and said: "Please do a stunt in the sky for us, Mr Musgrove!"

When he told them he would never do any more stunts, the children felt very sad and some even cried. Mr Musgrove could not bear to see little children sad, so he tied the radio set to the Helicopter, and jumping into the driving seat flew up into the air, to a burst of loud music.

"I'll do just one trick," he said to himself, "a new, and very special one!"

The children stopped crying and jumped up and down.

He flew high, high, high up into the sky till he was almost out of sight, then he came whizzing down and swooped low, low, low over the church steeple and away again.

The children, who had scrambled on to a nearby roof top to get a better view, cried: "It's a lovely trick! Do it again! PLEASE do it again!"

So Mr Musgrove flew high, high, high into the sky again and came whizzing and swooping down low, low low . . . But this time he came TOO low and . . . landed with a whizz! Wang! DONC! right on the church steeple.

The Postmaster-General, from his house on the hill, heard the crash and came galloping to the spot on his horse, Black Bertie. The Postal Authorities also heard the crash, and came running to the spot, on foot.

When he got to the church the Postmaster-General dismounted from Black Bertie and, waving his fist at Mr Musgrove, said sternly: "This is a very serious offence! Come down at once!"

"I can't," said Mr Musgrove, unhappily, ". . . I'm stuck!"

So the Postal Authorities got a ladder, climbed up the steeple, and lifted Mr Musgrove and the Helicopter down.

When they got to the ground, they examined Mr Musgrove's arms and legs and saw that nothing was broken. They also noticed that the radio set was intact. But the poor Helicopter was seriously damaged; its tail was drooping, its nose was pushed in, and its whole system was badly upset.

"It will take weeks to mend!" said the Postal Authorities.

The Postmaster-General turned to Mr Musgrove and said: "For this you will be dismissed from the Postal Service. Hand me your uniform."

Mr Musgrove sadly handed him his peaked hat and his little jacket that had red cord round the edges.

"Mr Boodle will take your place," said the Postmaster-General.

Mr Boodle was the Postman from the next village. He did not like the idea of delivering letters for two villages. "Too much for one man on a bicycle," he grumbled, but not loud enough for the Postmaster-General to hear.

Mr Musgrove went back to Fuchsia Cottage in his waistcoat.

"I've lost my job, Mrs Musgrove," he said.

Even Nina looked sad and her ears flopped forward.

"Never mind," said Mrs Musgrove, "we will think of a new job for you."

"I am not very good at doing anything except flying a Helicopter and delivering letters," said Mr Musgrove.

So they sat down to think and think, and Nina thought too, with her own special cow-like thoughts.

After a while Mrs Musgrove had a Plan.

"We will pick the strawberries from the back garden and

with the cream from Nina's milk we will make some Pink Ice Cream and sell it to people passing by," she cried.

"What a wonderful plan!" shouted Mr Musgrove, dancing happily round. "You *are* clever, Mrs Musgrove!"

Nina looked as if she thought it was a good idea, too, and said "Moo-oo!"

The next day Mr Musgrove went gaily into the back garden and picked a basketful of strawberries. He was careful not to eat any himself, but put them *all* into the

basket. Mrs Musgrove milked Nina and skimmed off the cream. And together they made some lovely Pink Ice Cream. Then they put up a notice:

PINK ICE CREAM FOR SALE

Nina looked very proud.

When the children saw the notice they ran eagerly in to buy. And even a few grown-ups came, and said, "Num, Num! What elegant Ice Cream!"

By evening they had sold out, so they turned the board round. Now it said:

PINK ICE CREAM TOMORROW

Every day they made more Pink Ice Cream and every evening they had sold out.

"We are beginning to make quite a lot of lovely money," said Mr Musgrove.

But though they were so successful with their Pink Ice Cream, Mr Musgrove often thought wistfully of the Helicopter, and his Postman's life. One day as he was exercising Nina in the woods, he met Mr Boodle. Mr Boodle grumbled that he had too much work to do.

"I would rather be a bicycling postman than no postman at all," sighed Mr Musgrove.

Early one morning before the Musgroves had opened their Ice Cream Stall, Nina saw the Postmaster-General riding along the road on his horse, Black Bertie. Nina liked Black Bertie, so as they passed she thrust her head through the fuchsia hedge and said, "Moo-oo."

Black Bertie was so surprised that he shied and reared up in the air . . . and tossed the Postmaster-General into the fuchsia hedge.

"Moo," said Nina, in alarm, and Mr and Mrs Musgrove came running up.

Carefully they carried him into the house. They laid him on a sofa and put smelling salts under his nose, and tried to make him take some strong, sweet tea, and a little brandy.

But nothing would revive him.

They tried practically everything, including chocolate biscuits and fizzy lemonade, but he never stirred, till Mrs Musgrove came towards him carrying a Pink Ice Cream.

"What's that?" he said, opening one eye. "It smells good."

So they gave him one.

"It's delicious!" he cried. "Delicious!"

They gave him another and another and another . . .

He ate SIX!

"I have recovered now," he said, standing up, "thanks to your elegant ice creams, which are the best I have ever tasted!"

Then he walked outside and called Black Bertie, who had walked into the garden and was eating the grass with Nina. "Come on, Black Bertie, we must go home," he said, and jumped into the saddle and rode away, waving his hand graciously to the Musgroves.

That afternoon, much to the Musgroves' surprise, he re-appeared. Nina was careful not to moo through the fuchsia hedge at Black Bertie this time.

"I have reappeared," said the Postmaster-General, "because I am so grateful for your kindness and your ice creams that I have prepared a little surprise for you up at my house. Would you like to come and see it, Mr Musgrove?"

"Why, yes!" cried Mr Musgrove, wondering excitedly what on earth it could be.

"Jump on, then!" cried the Postmaster-General. "I am afraid there isn't room for Mrs Musgrove too."

At first Mr Musgrove felt a bit nervous of Black Bertie, but he was too excited to see what the Postmaster-General's surprise was really to care.

When they arrived at the Postmaster-General's house they put Black Bertie away and gave him a piece of sugar. Then the Postmaster-General led Mr Musgrove up the steps of the house into the hall, where stood a large wooden chest. He opened the chest, and drew out . . . Mr Musgrove's peaked cap and little blue jacket with red cord round the edges!

He handed the uniform to Mr Musgrove. "Please wear this," he said, "and become once more the Flying Postman of Pagnum Moss!"

Mr Musgrove was very excited and thanked the Postmaster-General three times. Then the Postmaster-General took him out into the garden. "Look!" he said, pointing at the lawn, and there stood the Helicopter all beautifully mended!

"Jump in!" cried the Postmaster-General. "And be on duty tomorrow morning."

Mr Musgrove raced across the lawn and leapt gleefully in. As he was flying away the Postmaster-General called: "Will you sell me six of your beautiful Pink Ice Creams every day, and deliver them to me with the letters every morning?"

"Most certainly!" cried Mr Musgrove, leaning out of the Helicopter and saluting.

"Six Pink Ice Creams . . . I'll keep them in my refrigerator. Two for my lunch, two for my tea and two for my dinner!" shouted the Postmaster-General.

Imagine Mrs Musgrove's and Nina's surprise when Mr Musgrove alighted in the front garden, fully dressed in Postman's clothes.

"I'm a Postman again!" he cried. "Oh, happy day!"

"Moo-oo," said Nina, and Mrs Musgrove clapped her hands.

The next morning he set out to deliver letters and sing his song: "Wake up! Wake up! For morning is here!" and everyone woke up and shouted: "Mr Musgrove, the Flying Postman, is back in the sky again! Hurrah, Hooray!"

Mr Boodle, the grumbling postman, said, "Hurrah, Hooray!" too, because now he would not have so much work to do. He was so excited that he took his hands off the handlebars, and then he took his feet off the pedals till the Postmaster-General passed by and, pointing at him, said, "That is dangerous and silly."

So he put his hands back on the handlebars and his feet back on the pedals.

Mr Musgrove never forgot to bring the Postmaster-General the six Pink Ice Creams; two for his lunch, two for his tea and two for his dinner. And every day clever Mrs Musgrove made Pink Ice Cream all by herself, till soon they had enough money to buy a little Helicopter of their very own, which they called FLITTERMOUSE. They had Flittermouse made with a hollow in the back for Nina to sit in, and on Saturdays they went to the city to shop, and on Sundays they went for a spin.

Often Mr Musgrove did musical sky stunts in Flittermouse for the children, but he was careful never to fly low over the church steeple.

THE CHATTERBOX

A traditional Russian tale

There were once a man and his wife who lived in the middle of a village, in a pretty little cottage near the church. He was called John and she was called Mary. They hadn't been married long. They were very happy.

Well, the cottage made them happy. It was John's grandfather who'd planted the roses along the fence. And it was his great-grandfather who'd made the little front gate, where John and Mary stood in the evenings to watch their neighbours go by.

And it was their neighbours who made them happy. They'd known them all their lives. Standing by the front gate as the sun went down, they'd say, "Evening, Sarah! Evening, Tom! Evening, old Mrs Twistle! Evening, parson!"

And on Sundays they'd all go to church together, and it would be, "Morning, Sarah! Morning, John! Morning, Mary! Morning, old Mrs Twistle! Morning, parson!"

And John's work made them happy. He worked down on the great farm, that was owned by the lord of the place. He was a great lord indeed.

23

Everybody liked John and Mary. "Ah, they're a nice couple," people would say. "He's as nice as his old father was." "Ay, and *his* father before him." "And she's a good kind woman." "And her mother was a good kind woman, too." "Ay, and *her* mother before her." And so on.

BUT . . .

Though everyone thought Mary was a good kind woman – and she *was* – everyone also thought she was a chatterbox. She was a gossip. She was a tittle-tattle. You couldn't trust her with a secret.

So young Mrs Twistle, who was old Mrs Twistle's son's wife, would say, "Do you know what? My daughter Susan's thinking of getting married. You'll never guess who she's going to marry, Mary."

"Oh," Mary would say. "It must be that young man I've seen her with from the village the other side of the forest. Tom Trott – is that his name?"

"The very one," young Mrs Twistle would say. "She likes him and he likes her. And the long and short of it is they mean to get married in the spring. But it's a secret, Mary. They don't want anyone to know until Christmas. Young Tom wants to tell everybody at Christmas. You won't say a word to a soul, will you, Mary?"

And Mary would say of course not, she wouldn't say a word to anyone. The secret was safe with her. And she always meant it! Only . . . well, it was so exciting to have something secret to tell. And she'd meet Jenny Thrush, who was married to Jim Thrush, and she'd say, "Yes, my dear – married in the spring, she'll be, to that young fellow from the village on the other side of the forest. Tom Trott, that's his name." And then she'd remember her promise. "Oh dear," she'd say.

But by then it was too late.

So John and Mary were very happy, and all the time everybody liked John, and most of the time everybody liked Mary.

BUT . . .

Well, one evening, after work was over, John went into the forest. There were wolves about in those times, and John had found one of their dens, and he went along to dig it out. But he hadn't dug more than a foot into the ground when there was a *clink*. And another *clink*. And another . . .

Round things that went *clink*!

John picked one up and gave it a bit of a rub. My goodness! It was gold! It was treasure! It was a great heap of gold coins that someone had buried!

"Oh," thought John. "Now Mary and I can buy our own cow – and a bit of land of our own!" The ground was still going *clink* as he dug at it. "And I could buy Mary some pretty dresses!" *Clink, clink!* "But, of course, I'll have to keep it quiet. That lord of ours – if he got to hear of it, he'd want the gold for himself. He's got gold of his own, but he's a greedy man. We'll have to keep it quiet – both of us. Me and . . . Mary . . . Oh dear, oh dear! *Mary!* She'd never keep exciting news like this to herself."

What was he to do?

He was such a lucky man, he thought, but such an unlucky man too. Married to Mary, who was good and kind, and whom he loved. But a chatterbox!

He'd dug up all the coins now – there were hundreds of them – and then he'd buried them again. But how could he go home and tell Mary? She'd be bound to tell the next person she met. And that person would tell another person, and the lord would get to hear of it.

But then John had an idea!

He started on his way back home, and anybody who'd been watching would have been puzzled. Because John was dancing. He was dancing with delight. Because it was a wonderful idea he'd had!

Soon he came to the river. The day before he'd set a fish-net in the water. Now, when he pulled it out, he found a fine fish caught in it. So he took it out and off he went again.

A little further along, near the edge of the forest, he'd set a trap. There was a hare caught in it. He took out the hare and put the fish in the trap. Then he hurried back to the river and put the hare in the fish-net.

Then, still dancing with delight, he set off home. He went down the village street. "Evening, Sarah! Evening, Tom! Evening, old Mrs Twistle! Evening, parson!" And into his little cottage, where Mary was waiting for him.

"Oh, John, dear," she cried. "I wondered where you were – it's getting dark!" .

"Mary, my love," said John. "I want you to do something for me. I want you to heat up the oven and then bake me as many pancakes as you can."

"John, my dear husband!" cried Mary. "Whoever heard of anyone heating up the oven at this time of day! And who'd want to eat pancakes at bedtime! Even one pancake – let alone as many as I could bake!"

"Mary, my love," said John. "Don't argue! Oh, how can I tell you my news? The fact is we're rich! We're rich!"

"John! Dear John!" cried Mary.

"It's all right, my love," said John. "It's true! Digging in the forest I found a heap of gold . . ."

"Oh, John!"

"And we must bring it home in the darkness, so no one will see what we've got. Oh, Mary, my love, don't argue! It's gold! So warm the oven and bake the pancakes!"

"Gold! Oh, John! Oh, John! You shall have as many pancakes as you can eat, dear husband. No wonder you are hungry! Finding gold . . . !"

"That makes you hungry, Mary my love," said John.

And together they cried, *"Finding gold makes you hungry!"* And then they laughed with excitement.

So Mary warmed the oven and baked the pancakes. Though she was laughing so much she could hardly remember what she was doing.

"Here's the first lot, John, my dear," she said. "Eat them while they're hot, and I'll make some more."

And she was so excited that she didn't notice that John ate only one of the pancakes. The rest he slipped into his sack.

Soon she was back with more pancakes. Was that enough? Could they go and get the treasure now?

Not yet, said John, not yet. They mustn't go out and into the forest until the whole village was asleep.

So she made more pancakes, and still more. And every time John ate one, and slipped the rest into his sack. She couldn't make them fast enough. Ah, said John. It was a long way to go to where he'd buried the treasure, and the gold would be heavy to carry. He must give himself strength. More pancakes! And still more pancakes!

And at last his stomach was full, though his sack was even fuller. And off they set into the night.

John went first with his sack. Mary came after, trying not to laugh with excitement. She wanted to go and tell the whole world about the treasure John had found! She thought of all the dresses she'd buy: especially one she'd seen when the pedlar came round in the spring. It had ribbons! And she'd buy new shirts for John: especially some beautiful white ones for Sundays. She was so busy thinking of all this that she didn't notice what John was doing ahead of her in the darkness. He was feeling in his sack and taking out a pancake and slipping it over the branch of a tree. First one, and then another. A pancake on this branch, a pancake on that branch. Mary was thinking how they'd have a new chair made for old Mrs Twistle, when she suddenly caught sight of the pancakes.

"Growing on the trees!" she cried. "Pancakes! John, John! Have you ever seen that before?"

"What's that, my dear?" said John.

"There are pancakes growing on the trees," said Mary.

"Oh, they're not growing there, my love," said John. "Whoever heard of pancakes growing on trees! Didn't you see that great cloud of pancakes that went over some minutes ago?"

"A cloud of pancakes?"

"It was a very big one. It rained pancakes very hard for a moment. You must have been dreaming if you didn't notice."

"Oh, that's true, dear John," said Mary. "I was thinking what we'd do with our treasure!"

"Ah, Mary," said John, "what we'll do with our treasure! Yes! Well, we're nearly there. But . . . look! There's a trap I set not far from here, for a hare. Let's go and see what we've caught. Won't take a minute."

29

They left the path and made their way under the trees to where John had set his trap. "Here it is!" he cried. "Oh, Mary! How lucky we are! There's a fine fish in here!"

"A fish?" said Mary. "A fish in a trap you set for a hare? But how could a fish get into such a trap? We're nowhere near the river yet, John."

"Sssh, Mary, my love," said John. "Don't get excited! Even here, someone might hear us! Didn't you know there are fish that can walk?"

"Oh, I'd never have believed it," said Mary. "Fish that can walk! Well, well!"

And soon they could hear water. They were near the river. John said, "I've a net somewhere here. Let's stop for a moment and see if we've caught anything in that." They made their way under the trees to the river bank. "Ah," cried John. "Here it is! And my goodness – a hare! A fine fat hare caught in my net! That's a good thing, my dear! We may have found gold, but we'll still be glad of a fine hare for Sunday dinner, won't we?"

"But what is the world coming to?" said Mary. "A hare in a fish-net? A hare in the river? How can that be?"

"Mary, my dear," said John. "You're the sweetest of wives, but you know very little of the world. You've never seen pancakes in trees, you've never heard of a walking fish, and now you've never heard of a water-hare!"

"A water-hare?" said Mary. "Is that what it is?"

"Of course it is," said John. "Well, on we go."

And at last they came to a tree with a scratch on it. John had marked it so he would be able to find the gold. And he took his spade, and dug – and there was the treasure. And he filled his sack with the gold – there was plenty of room, now the pancakes were gone.

And then, as happy as two people ever were, they made their way home.

Well, yes, they were happy. But in the darkness, poor Mary jumped at every sound. They were nearly home and passing near the lord's great house when they heard the bleating of his sheep.

"Oh, John," cried Mary. "Dear John! What's that? What's that terrible noise?"

"Run, dear Mary!" cried John. "Run for your life! It's the little bad creatures that live in the forest. They must have got into our lord's house and are pinching him black and blue, poor man! Run!"

And they ran and they ran until they reached the village. They ran up the street, past the church, into their cottage. They stowed the bag of gold under the bed. Then they leapt into bed themselves, and were soon fast asleep. That is after John had sleepily said, "Remember, my love, not a word to a soul about our treasure!"

And Mary had sleepily replied, "Of course, dear husband. I wouldn't dream of saying a word to anyone!"

And Mary meant it! Not a word would she say! Not even to her dearest friend! Especially not to her dearest friend, who lived in the cottage across the street! Especially not to her dearest friend, to whom she always told everything!

Though nothing she'd ever told her dearest friend had been half as exciting as what she now had to . . . What she now had *not* to tell!

NOT to tell!

NOT to tell!

Not even to her dearest friend!

Next morning, she was across the road and sitting in her dearest friend's kitchen. "Such news," she was saying. (And she was yawning! Well, it *had* been a late night!) "But I can't tell you anything about it!"

"You're very tired this morning, Mary!" said her dearest friend.

"So would you be if you'd been up half the . . . Oh!" said Mary.

"Up half the night, you mean?" asked her friend. "Oh, Mary, what *is* it?"

"Oh, it's such a vexation that I can't tell you," said Mary. "And it isn't as if it's every day one's husband digs up a great heap of gold!"

"Gold!"

"Oh, oh," said Mary. "What have I said?"

What *had* she said! To her dearest friend – who was soon speaking to *her* dearest friend – who spoke to old Mrs Twistle – who spoke to the blacksmith – who spoke to his wife – who spoke to her married daughter – who told her husband – who told the shepherd – who spoke to old Mr Twistle – who'd already heard it from his wife *and* from Mary – who'd also told the forester's wife – who'd told the parson's wife – who'd told the parson . . . And the parson had told the lord himself, up at the great house.

"What's that!" the lord cried. "Have them sent here, man and wife! We'll get to the bottom of this! Treasure found in the forest is *my* treasure! Have them brought at once! I've never heard of such a thing!"

He said a lot more, and all of it angry. Any gold found in those parts was *his* gold! "*Grrrh!*" he said, and his face was red with anger.

And so, up to the great house went John and his trembling wife. And the lord began shouting again.

"How dare you!" he roared. "How dare you keep gold found in the forest to yourself! I'll have you whipped! I'll have you turned out of your cottage! I'll have you – oh, nothing's bad enough for you." He glared at John. "Well, man – say something!"

"My lord," said John, "what is there for me to say, except that I know nothing of any treasure? It's some strange mistake . . . some . . ."

"Don't try to deceive me!" cried the lord. "It's useless to deny it! Everyone in the village knows about it. And how do they know about it? Because your wife here told them about it!"

33

"My wife!" cried John. "My dear wife! Ah, my lord, now I understand. She's a good woman – ask anyone in the village – and I love her dearly. But, my lord, there's no believing a thing she says. She's . . . Er . . ." He went closer to the lord and spoke in a whisper. "She's rather silly, my lord. She imagines things. She's . . . ah . . . a little . . . ah . . . you understand me, my lord?"

"I understand that you're an impudent fellow," said the lord. "Do you think you can get away with a story like that? Now, hold your tongue while I speak to your wife. If I'm not mistaken, I'll soon get the truth from her!" He turned to Mary. "Now, tell me, good woman, did your husband not find a treasure?"

"Oh yes, my lord," said Mary, who was still trembling. "Indeed he did."

"And where did he find it?"

"In the forest, my lord."

"Ah, and you went to fetch it?"

"Yes, at night, my lord."

"At night? Why at night?"

"Because, my lord, my dear John said – oh dear – "

"What did he say?"

"He said if you knew of it you'd take it from us!"

The lord roared like an elephant.

"Ah, the truth!" he cried. "I knew we'd get it. Take your time, woman, and tell the whole story. Tell me what happened, step by step."

"Well, my lord," said Mary, "we went into the forest, and – it was the night it rained pancakes."

"The night it did what?"

"I thought the pancakes were growing on the trees, my lord! What a silly woman I was! I didn't notice the cloud of pancakes as it passed overhead."

"You didn't notice the . . . ! What happened then?"

"Oh, after that we looked in one of my husband's traps, my lord, and there was a fish in it."

"There was a *what?*"

"It was silly, my lord – I mean, I was silly. Can you believe it, but I didn't know that fish could walk. At least, as your lordship will know, not being a silly woman, *some* fish can walk."

"Some fish can – *what?*" The lord growled like a dog.

"You'll not believe it, but I was even surprised when we came to the river and found a hare in my husband's fish-net."

The lord couldn't speak. His face was becoming redder and redder.

Mary laughed. "It was a water-hare, of course," she said. "Can you believe it, my lord – I didn't even know there were hares that lived in the river." She laughed even louder. "And I didn't even know about the bad little creatures that come out of the forest and pinch your lordship black and blue in the night. We heard them, it was horrible, as we came home. And that reminds me, your lordship – I should have asked you before – how *is* your lordship? Not too badly hurt, I hope? I just hope they don't come and pinch you every night!"

The lord spluttered.

"Oh," said Mary, "I've forgotten the most important thing, my lord. After we'd found the hare in the river, we found the gold. It was in a hole in the ground, and – "

"Don't tell me any more," said the lord. "There were lots and lots of gold pieces . . ."

"Oh yes, my lord," said Mary.

"And you picked them up and took them home."

"Oh yes, my lord."

"Oh, don't tell me any more," said the lord. Even his ears were red with rage. "I'm not a fool, you know. Your story is worthless, woman. You're a silly creature. I'm sorry for your husband. Off with you both, before I lose my temper!" (If he hadn't lost his temper already, John thought, why were his ears so red?) "And let no one bring me any more ridiculous stories about finding gold told by silly women."

"You see, my lord," said John. "It's as I said. You can't believe a word that passes her lips. But she is a dear kind soul, for all that."

Mary never did understand what had happened. I think some of their friends in the village began to understand, when they thought it over. And they probably smiled to themselves. Well, you were always sure of a good meal or something good to drink if you visited John and Mary in their cottage. They seemed to live very comfortably. Mary had some very nice dresses, and no one had whiter shirts on Sundays than John.

And everyone thought Mary was very good. And very kind. And a good wife to John. It was just that . . .

Well, as old Mrs Twistle said, she was a gossip, and a tittle-tattle – and a *chatterbox*.

HOW THE HEDGEHOG BEAT THE OSTRICH

A tale from the Sahara

People who live in deserts have to move about a lot. They must go wherever there's food for their animals. Camels, goats, sheep – they need to eat, and in a desert the food is sometimes here, sometimes there, but not often in one particular place that you can depend on. Except when you see that it's going to rain.

When the rain is on its way, the people of the desert may sow barley, here or there. And then, at harvest time, they come back and reap it.

Well, there was a barley field in the Sahara. That, as you know, is one of the greatest deserts of all. It was growing, the barley, inch by inch, and soon the people would return, to harvest it. Meanwhile, here was Hedgehog and here was Ostrich. They'd met by the field: and as far as someone very tall could talk to someone very small, they were talking.

"It must be very hard," said Ostrich, "when you're only half as high as a stalk of barley!"

Hedgehog thought that wasn't a very polite remark. "I'm small," he said. "You're quite right about that. But then I can run faster than anyone else in the Sahara."

Ostrich could hardly believe his ears. "Faster than anyone else in the Sahara!" he cried. "My dear small prickly friend! I am without doubt one of the fastest creatures in the whole world! Well, you've only to look at my legs!" And he smiled down at those long, strong legs of his. "They are perhaps the very best legs ever, for running," he said.

"Oh yes," said Hedgehog. "I see. That's what *you* think. Well, what about this? Suppose we see who's quickest at counting the rows of barley in this field?"

"My goodness," said Ostrich. "I'm afraid there's no doubt who would come out best there!" He ran a few yards, just to show Hedgehog what he was up against. "World class, you see," he said.

"But you will race against me?" asked Hedgehog.

"My dear friend, of course," said Ostrich.

So they agreed to run against each other next day. Meanwhile, they went round to their friends, inviting them to be present at the race.

Before the sun got too high, they met at the barley field. Ostrich looked very confident. Hedgehog looked very serious. Ostrich's friends were standing round the field, ready to cheer him on. There wasn't a sign of Hedgehog's friends. Well, thought Ostrich, they were too *tiny*, he guessed, to be seen over the top of the barley. Funny little fellows, hedgehogs!

They stood together, looked at each other and at a wink of Ostrich's great eye, off they went. Hedgehog vanished at once, smaller than the stalks of barley. Ostrich took his great steps across the field, still smiling. "One – two – three – four – five . . ." he shouted, as he left one row after another behind him.

And to his horror, he heard the voice of Hedgehog calling, "Three – four – five – six – seven . . ."

Ostrich couldn't believe it! But he began to quicken his stride. "Six – seven – eight – nine – ten . . ." he shouted.

"Nine – ten – eleven – twelve – thirteen . . ." came Hedgehog's voice, ahead of him.

Ostrich was no longer smiling. His great legs flew across the field. "Fourteen – fifteen – sixteen . . ." he shouted.

There were twenty-one rows of barley in that field. "Twenty-one!" cried Ostrich, and his friends rushed up to congratulate him.

But *there* was Hedgehog. He was sitting quietly on a little hill of sand at the end of the field, and clearly he'd got there first. Hedgehog had won.

Ostrich was terribly upset. He couldn't understand it. In all the excitement, and feeling so angry as he did, he never asked himself again where all Hedgehog's friends, all those other hedgehogs, had been while the race was going on. It never struck him that only hedgehogs can really tell one hedgehog from another.

DON'T
CUT THE LAWN!

Margaret Mahy

Mr Pomeroy went to his seaside cottage for the holidays. The sea was right, the sand was right, the sun was right, the salt was right. But outside his cottage the lawn had grown into a terrible, tussocky tangle. Mr Pomeroy decided that he would have to cut it.

He got out his lawnmower, Snapping Jack.

"Now for some fun!" said Snapping Jack. "Things have been very quiet lately. I've been wanting to get at that cheeky grass for weeks and weeks."

Mr Pomeroy began pushing the lawnmower, and the grass flew up and out. However, he had gone only a few steps when out of the tangly, tussocky jungle flew a lark crying:

"Don't cut the lawn, don't cut the lawn!
You will cut my little nestlings which have just been born."

Mr Pomeroy went to investigate and there, sure enough, were four baby larks in a nest on the ground.

"No need to worry, Madam!" cried Mr Pomeroy to the anxious mother. "We will go around your nest and cut the lawn further away."

So they went around the nest and started cutting the lawn further away.

"Now for it!" said Snapping Jack, snapping away happily.
But just then out jumped a mother hare crying:
"Don't cut the lawn, don't cut the lawn!
You will cut my little leveret which has just been born."
Mr Pomeroy went to investigate and there, sure enough,
was a little brown leveret, safe in his tussocky form.

"We'll have to go further away to do our mowing," Mr
Pomeroy said to Snapping Jack. So they went further away
and Mr Pomeroy said, "Now we'll really begin cutting this
lawn."

"Right!" said Snapping Jack. "And we'll have no mercy
on it."

But they had only just begun to have no mercy on the lawn when a tabby cat leaped out of the tussocky tangle and mewed at them:

"Don't cut the lawn, don't cut the lawn!
You will cut my little kittens which have just been born."

Mr Pomeroy went to investigate, and there, sure enough, were two stripy kittens in a little, golden, tussocky, tangly hollow.

"This place is more like a zoo than a lawn," grumbled Snapping Jack. "We'll go further away this time, but you must promise to be hard-hearted or the lawn will get the better of us."

"All right! If it happens again I'll be very hard-hearted," promised Mr Pomeroy.

They began to cut where the lawn was longest, lankiest, tangliest and most terribly tough and tussocky.

"I'm not going to take any notice of any interruptions this time," he said to himself firmly.

"We'll really get down to business," said Snapping Jack, beginning to champ with satisfaction.

Then something moved in the long, lank, tussocky tangle. Something slowly sat up and stared at them with jewelled eyes. It was a big mother dragon, as green as grass, as golden as a tussock. She looked at them and she hissed:

"Don't cut the lawn, don't cut the lawn!
You will cut my little dragon who has just been born."

There, among the leathery scraps of the shell of the dragon's egg, was a tiny dragon, as golden and glittering as a bejewelled evening bag. It blew out a tiny flame àt them, just like a cigarette lighter.

"Isn't he clever for one so young!" exclaimed his loving mother. "Of course I can blow out a very big flame. I could

43

burn all this lawn in one blast if I wanted to. I could easily scorch off your eyebrows."

"Fire restrictions are on," croaked the alarmed Mr Pomeroy.

"Oh, I'm afraid that wouldn't stop me," said the dragon. "Not if I were upset about anything. And if you mowed my baby I'd be very upset. I'd probably breathe fire hot enough to melt a lawnmower!"

"What do *you* think?" Mr Pomeroy asked Snapping Jack.

"Let's leave it until next week," said Snapping Jack hurriedly. "We don't want to upset a loving mother, do we? Particularly one that breathes fire!"

So the lawn was left alone and Mr Pomeroy sat on his verandah enjoying the sun, or swam in the sea enjoying the salt water, and day by day he watched the cottage lawn grow more tussocky and more tangly. Then, one day, out of the tussocks and tangles flew four baby larks which began learning how to soar and sing as larks do. And out of the tussocks and tangles came a little hare which frolicked and frisked as hares do. And out of the tussocks and tangles came two stripy kittens which pounced and bounced as kittens do. And *then* out of the tussocks and tangles came a little dragon with golden scales and eyes like stars, and it laid its shining head on Mr Pomeroy's knee and told him some of the wonderful stories that only dragons know. Even Snapping Jack listened with interest.

"Fancy that!" he was heard to remark. "I'm glad I talked Mr Pomeroy out of mowing the lawn. Who'd ever believe a tussocky, tangly lawn could be home to so many creatures. There's more to a lawn than mere grass, you know!"

And Mr Pomeroy, the larks, the leveret, the kittens and the little dragon all agreed with him.

THE LITTLE POT AND THE FLOOD OF PORRIDGE

A tale from Germany

There was once a poor widow who had a little cottage, a *very* little garden, and a daughter. They ate what they could grow in the garden and when summer came, the daughter would go into the wood and pick wild strawberries.

She was doing that one bright day, and had had a good morning. Her basket was half-full already. It was time for lunch. So she sat on a fallen tree and prepared to eat the piece of bread she'd brought with her. She thought she might eat a few wild strawberries too. There was a little brook nearby, with clear sweet water running in it. She'd drink from that when she was ready.

And at that moment, as it seemed out of nowhere, an old woman appeared. She was very small, and had a hunched back and a kindly face. She was holding a little pot.

"Oh, my darling," she said, in a little fluty sort of voice. "I'm *so* hungry! I have eaten nothing since the day before the day before the day before yesterday. Would you give me a bite of that bread in your hand?"

"It's rather hard bread – we can't afford anything better," said the girl. "But of course you can have some. Indeed, take it all. I shall soon be going home, and I can eat there. But mind your teeth. It *is* hard!"

"Bless you, my darling," said the old woman. "You're a good, kind girl. But I must give you something for it. Here, take this pot. It's a rather special pot. You've only got to say, 'Little pot, what about some porridge?' and at once it will cook porridge for you. And when the pot is full, you must say, 'Little pot, that's enough!' and it will stop. But you must remember the exact words. No other words will do. Alas, it wouldn't work for me. That is why I am so hungry. But for you, I know it will work."

And the old woman bit into the bread, hard though it was, handed over the little pot, and vanished as she had come.

When the girl arrived home she showed her mother first the basket full of wild strawberries, and then the mysterious little pot. Feeling very excited, they placed the pot on the table and the girl said, "Little pot, what about some porridge?" The pot had been absolutely empty, but now, from the bottom of it, porridge came bubbling. A little porridge, and then a little more, and then a lot of porridge, till the pot was full. Then the girl said, "Little pot, that's enough!" and at once the pot stopped producing porridge. And the widow and her daughter fetched their spoons and – my, that was *good* porridge! It was good, sweet porridge! Not for a long time had they felt so contented after a meal.

The next day (after they'd had guess-what for breakfast), the girl went off again to pick wild strawberries. She hadn't been gone long before the widow felt hungry again. So she put the pot on the table and said, "Little pot, what about some porridge?" And to her joy, it worked for her too. At once the little pot began filling with thick, wholesome, sweet porridge.

Now the old woman's porridge bowl, and her spoon, were out in the kitchen, where they'd been washed up after

breakfast. So the widow trotted out to get them, and when she returned – oh my! The porridge was pouring out of the pot. Actually, it had poured out of the pot on to the table, and off the table on to a chair, and off the chair on to the floor, and now it was pouring across the floor. The widow was so horrified she couldn't remember the words that would make the little pot stop.

"Oh, little pot, please don't!" she cried. "Please, you awkward little pot, *that will do!*" she cried again, and then, "Oh please, pot – please, *please*, PLEASE!"

But the pot paid no attention, for those were quite the wrong words. The widow tried to stop the porridge by covering the bowl with a cloth. But the porridge simply pushed the cloth out of the way, and now in the room there

was a kind of flood of porridge. It had covered the floor, and was rising up the walls, and if the widow had stayed she'd have suffered a very strange death. She'd have drowned in porridge, which not many people do. But she ran up the stairs to the bedroom and then, as the porridge began to climb the stairs, she pulled herself up into the loft.

By now the porridge had forced open the front door of the cottage, and the back door, and was pouring out into the little garden, and into the street. It broke the windows, too, and poured out of them. The street was soon a river of porridge, and the village green had become a great porridge pond. And some people who'd been out of doors when this happened had to climb trees, or they would have been up to their waists in porridge. And still it came. The widow had

climbed out of the topmost window and on to the roof. But still the level of the porridge rose.

And at that moment, thank goodness, the widow's daughter appeared. She had filled her basket with wild strawberries in record time. As soon as she saw what was happening, she called out, "Little pot, that's enough!"

And the pot stopped cooking porridge.

I'm afraid the widow had to stay on the roof of the cottage and the villagers had to stay up the trees until they got rid of all that porridge. Which they did only when all the other villagers got together and ate their way through it, until there was only a little porridge left. And they all had dreadful indigestion.

After which, they had to clean the place again. As someone said, it was the first time they'd ever had a whole village to wash up.

HOW THE FROG FROM OSAKA MET THE FROG FROM KYOTO

A Japanese tale

This is the tale of two Japanese frogs. One lived in a rather small pond in the city of Osaka, which is by the sea. The other lived in a rather narrow ditch in the city of Kyoto, which is not by the sea. They were both perfectly happy, except for one thing. The frog living in Osaka was always wondering what the city of Kyoto was like. And every now and then the frog living in Kyoto would say to himself, "I wonder what sort of place Osaka is?"

One day, and it happened to be the same day, neither of them could bear it any more. The frog in Osaka woke and thought, "I *must* make the journey to Kyoto!" And the frog in Kyoto woke and thought, "I *must* make the journey to Osaka!" And they both sighed. Well, one was very comfortable in his rather small pond, and the other was thoroughly at home in his rather narrow ditch. But how could you live in Osaka all your life and never know what it was like in Kyoto? And how could you live all your life in Kyoto and never know what it was like in Osaka!

So off they went, on their long hopping journeys. They hopped for dusty mile after dusty mile. They hopped along sunny lanes. They hopped across rice-fields. Suddenly it rained all over Japan, and they hopped through thousands of puddles. They hopped through villages. And at the very same moment when the frog from Osaka came to the foot of

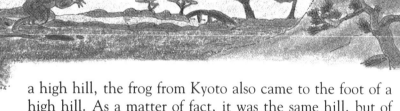

a high hill, the frog from Kyoto also came to the foot of a high hill. As a matter of fact, it was the same hill, but of course, one was on the side nearest to Osaka, and the other was on the side nearest to Kyoto. And hopping rather wearily, each climbed to the top.

And there they met.

Imagine that! They stretched themselves under a tree with their legs spread comfortably behind them. Oh, how nice to have a rest from all that hopping! And, of course, they talked.

"I'm from Osaka," said the frog from Osaka. "I live in a rather small pond, but if ever you find yourself in that part of the world, you'd be very welcome to stay. Plenty of flies, and rather nice muddy water. Oh, I wouldn't mind being back there!" And as he thought of his pond, and his friends, and all that marvellous mud, his huge bright frog's eyes filled with tears.

"And I'm from Kyoto," said the frog from Kyoto. He stretched his weary legs and sighed. "I live in a rather

narrow ditch, but if ever you visit the city, do come and spend a day or two with me. We've lots of flies, too, and some particularly muddy mud. Oh, I do wish I was home again!" And as he thought of his ditch, and his friends, and that particularly muddy mud, there were tears in his beautiful green and yellow eyes.

"May I ask why you've left home?" said the frog from Osaka.

"Oh, I thought I must go and see the city of Osaka," said the frog from Kyoto. "But what are you doing on the top of this hill?"

"Oh, I couldn't be happy until I'd had a look at the city of Kyoto," said the frog from Osaka.

Well, you can imagine their surprise! Fancy a frog from Osaka, going to Kyoto, meeting a frog from Kyoto, going to Osaka! And on top of a hill!

"Oh, what a pity!" said the frog from Kyoto. "If you think of it, being on the top of a hill, I ought to be able to see Osaka from here. And you ought to be able to see Kyoto. In the distance, of course. Very far away. Looking very small. But we could see enough to decide if it was worth going on. But we're not tall enough."

"It's the trouble with being a frog," said the frog from Osaka. "Don't get me wrong. I like being a frog."

"It's a good thing, being a frog," said the frog from Kyoto.

"But," said the frog from Osaka, "we're not tall enough to see things in the distance."

"Wait a minute," said the frog from Kyoto. "Tell me what you think about this. Suppose we stand up, leaning against each other . . ."

"Balancing on our back legs," said the frog from Osaka.

"Holding on to each other's front legs."

"So we don't fall over."

"Then I could look at Osaka! Over there in the distance!"

"And I," said the frog from Osaka, "could look at Kyoto, somewhere in the distance over there!"

"Shall we try it?" asked the frog from Kyoto.

"Let's try it," said the frog from Osaka.

So they tried it. Very carefully. First they moved as close as they could. Then they raised themselves on their strong back legs, their hopping legs. Then they leaned against each other, one set of front legs braced against the other. And it worked! Suddenly, instead of being two frogs flat on the ground, they were two tall frogs standing, able to see into the distance.

So they looked.

The frog from Osaka looked, as he thought, at the city of Kyoto. And the frog from Kyoto, as he thought, looked at the city of Osaka. And both of them croaked with dismay.

"Oh, how disappointing!" cried the frog from Osaka.

"Oh, what a disappointment!" cried the frog from Kyoto.

"What can you see?" asked the frog from Osaka.

"I see Osaka," said the frog from Kyoto. "But it's exactly the same as Kyoto. And what do you see?"

"I see Kyoto," said the frog from Osaka. "But it's exactly the same as Osaka."

And so they let themselves down on to the ground again. And they lay there sighing. All that hopping, through all those lanes, and puddles, and villages, and rice-fields! And

Kyoto turned out to be exactly like Osaka, and Osaka turned out to be exactly like Kyoto.

"Well, I'm not going any further," said the frog from Osaka. "I'm going back to my pond."

"And I'm not going any further," said the frog from Kyoto. "I'm going back to my ditch."

And so, as well as frogs could, they bowed to each other. Well, you know how the Japanese always bow when they meet and when they part. In this respect, Japanese frogs are just like Japanese people. And then they turned and went home – the frog from Osaka, of course, to Osaka, and the frog from Kyoto, of course, to Kyoto.

Now, I'm not going to say frogs are stupid. They are not. But those two frogs had forgotten something. They'd forgotten they were different from other animals not only in not being tall. Frogs, you remember, have their eyes at the top of their heads. And so, when they stood balanced against each other –

Do you see what I mean?

The frog from Osaka was looking backwards at Osaka. No wonder he thought it looked just like Osaka – it *was* Osaka. And the frog from Kyoto was looking backwards at Kyoto. No wonder he thought it looked just like Kyoto – it *was* Kyoto.

I must say they were glad to get back to their friends, and the flies they were fond of eating, and their marvellous muddy mud. But from that time on, if you asked the frog from Osaka about Kyoto, he'd grumble, "Not worth a visit! It's so like Osaka, you can't tell the difference!"

And ask the frog from Kyoto about Osaka, and he'd croak, "Don't go there! All they've done is copy Kyoto."

And as he hopped away you'd sometimes hear him grumble, "Copycats!"

BRAINBOX

Philippa Pearce

Once upon a time a horse lived by himself in a large meadow. His name was Brainbox; but he was not really a clever horse at all. In his meadow Brainbox had grass to eat and a stream to drink from; but he had no company. He felt very lonely. He needed another horse to be his friend.

One day Brainbox could bear his loneliness no longer. He trotted to the far end of his meadow; then he turned and began to canter, then to gallop towards the other end. He galloped as fast as he could – faster and faster – until he reached the hedge, and then he JUMPED. He cleared the hedge, jumping right out of his meadow altogether and into the lane on the other side.

"This is a lane," said Brainbox to himself. "If I go along it, perhaps I shall find another horse to be my friend." He began to trot down the lane. As he went, he kept a sharp look-out for another horse.

One thing was worrying Brainbox: he was not certain of recognizing another horse if he saw one. He had lived alone in his meadow for so long that he could not remember what other horses looked like. "And if I can't remember that," said Brainbox to himself, "then I've nothing to go on, have I?" He was not a very clever horse.

He was not clever, but he was determined. "I shall just have to ask," said Brainbox. "Ask and ask and ask again."

The first creature he saw in the lane was a snake – a harmless grass-snake. The snake was gliding among the grasses at the side of the lane.

Brainbox called: "Wait, you there!"

The snake paused a moment.

"Are you a horse?" asked Brainbox. "Because I'm looking for a horse to be my friend."

The snake gazed at him in amazement. "Sssssilly – sssso ssssilly!" hissed the snake. "Can't you see I'm not a horse? I'm a snake."

"How can one tell the difference?" asked Brainbox.

"Horses have legs, for one thing," said the snake. "Snakes haven't – they don't need them. Watch!" And, legless, the snake glided swiftly away and out of sight among the grasses.

"Well, now, that's a useful bit of information, for a start," said the not-so-very-clever Brainbox. "Now I know that I have to find a creature with legs, if I'm to find a horse to be my friend."

And he trotted on down the lane.

The next creature he saw in the lane was a hen who had strayed from her hen-run. She was pecking about in the lane when the horse caught sight of her. She pecked here at a seed, there at an insect, and as she pecked she ran to and fro. "On legs!" said Brainbox to himself. So he called out: "You there, with the legs! Are you a horse? I'm looking for a horse to be my friend."

The hen cackled, "Bad luck! Bad luck! Bad luck! I'm a hen, not a horse, can't you see?"

"But you've got legs!" said Brainbox.

"And I've got wings, too – look!" said the hen; and she stretched her wings and flapped them. "Hens have wings; horses haven't."

"No winged horses?"

"No. Hens, yes; horses, no."

"Pity," said Brainbox. To himself he thought: this question of wings or not-wings complicates everything. He decided not to think about wings or not-wings, but to concentrate only on legs.

Aloud, he said to the hen: "All the same, you could be a horse, couldn't you? You have legs."

"But only two," said the hen. "Hens have two legs; horses have four legs. Hens, two legs; horses, four legs. Hens, two; horses, four."

"So I need an animal with four legs if I want a horse to be my friend?" said Brainbox. He just wanted to check.

But the hen had seen a beetle in the grass. Without waiting to answer, she scuttled away after it, and Brainbox was left alone.

"Four legs . . ." he said to himself. He decided that he was sure he was right, even without the hen's saying so. "Four legs . . ." he repeated, memorizing the information. "Four legs . . . four legs . . ."

He began once more to trot down the lane.

The next animal he came upon was a dog who had just found an old bone. The dog was gnawing his bone, so Brainbox had time to look at him closely. Brainbox saw that the dog had legs. He counted them: one – two – three – four –

"I say!" he cried joyfully. "You've four legs – I've counted them! Exactly four! So, please – you are a horse, aren't you? I'm looking for a horse to be my friend."

The dog almost fell over with laughter; he even dropped his bone. Then he began barking madly at Brainbox: "Wruff! Wruff! Stuff and nonsense! Of course, I'm not a horse – I'm a dog – a dog – a dog!"

"But you've four legs," argued Brainbox. "Why shouldn't you be a horse?"

"My legs are dogs' legs," said the dog. "Quite different from horses' legs. For one thing, dogs' legs end in paws – look, like mine! Horses' legs end in hoofs, like yours. Legs with hoofs, that's what you want." And the dog picked up his bone and went off elsewhere to gnaw it undisturbed.

"I'm getting a more exact picture," said Brainbox to himself. "I must find a creature with legs, four of them, and hoofs at the end of the legs. Then I've found a horse to be my friend."

And he trotted off down the lane.

Further down the lane he met a sheep who was wandering up it, browsing on the wayside grasses as it went. When the sheep heard the horse coming, it lifted its head to stare.

"Legs," said Brainbox to himself. "And one – two – three – four of them. And each ends in – yes, in a little hoof!" He said aloud to the sheep: "Please, tell me: aren't you a horse? You've legs – four of them – and four hoofs as well. Surely

you're a horse? I want to find a horse to be my friend."

The sheep stared and stared. Then it said: "Baaaa! Baaaarmy – that's what you are! I'm a sheep; not a horse!"

"But your legs have hoofs!"

"Not like a horse's hoofs. Look at my hoofs – "

"I did," said Brainbox, "when I counted your legs."

"Now look at your own hoofs."

"Why should I look at my own hoofs?"

"You're a horse, aren't you?" said the sheep.

"What's that got to do with it?" said Brainbox, confused.

The sheep stared and stared. It bleated something to itself which Brainbox did not catch. Then it said: "A sheep's hoofs are cloven. A horse's aren't." And the sheep turned its back on Brainbox and began browsing again.

"Well," said Brainbox, trying to cheer himself up, "I'm getting nearer all the time. Legs; four of them; hoofs at the end of the legs; hoofs not cloven. Find all that, and I've found a horse to be my friend."

And he trotted off down the lane.

Further down the lane he met a donkey. They looked at each other. The horse saw that the donkey had legs. He counted them: one – two – three – four. He looked at the end of each leg: a hoof. He looked at the hoofs: uncloven.

Then Brainbox shouted at the donkey. "At last! You're a horse! And I've been looking for a horse to be my friend."

"Eeeyore! You're a fool!" said the donkey. "I'm a donkey, not a horse."

"But you have everything," Brainbox insisted. "Legs, four of them; hoofs, uncloven. *Why* aren't you a horse?"

"I've told you," said the donkey. "Because I'm a donkey."

Brainbox could have cried with disappointment. He stood, baffled and woebegone, in the middle of the lane, his head drooping almost to the ground in his despair. He did not know what to do next.

In the end, he begged the donkey to listen to the sad story of his search and advise him, and the donkey agreed. Then Brainbox told him all about his meeting with the snake and the hen and the dog and the sheep, and their helpful remarks. "So you see," said Brainbox, "I thought I could *work out* what a horse would look like. At least, I'd got the legs right."

"There's a lot more to a horse than a set of legs," said the donkey.

"I daresay," said Brainbox; "but I don't know any more. It all comes back to the fact that I've quite forgotten what other horses look like. I've got nothing to go on."

"You've something to go on," said the donkey. "You are a horse."

"Someone else said that to me," said Brainbox, puzzled. "They seemed to think it made a difference in some way."

"It does," said the donkey. "You know what another horse will look like."

"What will it look like?"

"Like you."

Brainbox was thunderstruck. "Like me . . ." He turned the idea over in his mind: it was new; it had possibilities; it might work.

"For instance," said the donkey, "look at your tail. Then look at mine."

Brainbox looked over his shoulder at his tail, and swished it. He looked at it carefully, as he had never bothered to do before, and saw that his tail was made up of a great number of very long, strong hairs. Then he looked at the donkey's tail: it looked rather like an old-fashioned bell-pull, with just a tuft of hairs at the end.

"Yes," said Brainbox, "I can see that our tails are quite different." He looked at the rest of the donkey, and then at as much of himself as he could see. He said, "I don't look very much like you at all, except perhaps for the legs."

"It's not just looks either," said the donkey. "A horse will have a special voice, just like your voice; and he'll have a special horse-smell, just like yours; and – and – well, when you meet another horse, you'll *know* he's a horse just because you're a horse, too."

"And you think I really might meet another horse?"

"I do," said the donkey.

"Then I'd best be off again," said Brainbox. "Thank you very much indeed for your advice." And he began trotting down the lane, in the direction from which the donkey had just come.

"Eeeyore!" the donkey called after him. "You're going to be lucky!"

Brainbox wondered what the donkey meant.

At the end of the lane, Brainbox came to a five-barred gate. A creature stood on the other side of the gate, with its head hanging over the top bar, looking sad. Brainbox saw that the creature was four-legged, with uncloven hoofs and a tail of long, strong hairs. But it wasn't just the creature's looks that excited Brainbox. The creature's smell was pleasantly familiar; and just when Brainbox was wondering what the voice would sound like, the creature lifted his head, looked straight at Brainbox, and said: "Neigh! neigh! The name's Dobbin. What's yours?"

"Brainbox," said Brainbox. "I'm a horse; and I *know* you're a horse, too. Why do you look so miserable?"

Dobbin said: "I live alone in this meadow, and I feel very lonely sometimes. There's no other horse to be my friend."

"Wait there!" said Brainbox. He turned round and began to trot back up the lane, the way he had come. The donkey, who saw him approaching, called out, "You're going in the wrong direction!"

"No, I'm not," said Brainbox. "You wait and see."

He trotted on past the donkey and then past the sheep and past the dog and past the hen and past the grass-snake. They all stopped what they were doing to stare, when they heard the sound of horse's hoofs approaching.

When he judged that he had gone far enough, Brainbox turned and began to trot back towards the five-barred gate at the end of the lane.

He trotted faster and faster –
   past the grass-snake,
   past the hen –
– faster and faster, until he was cantering –
   past the dog,
   past the sheep –
– faster and faster, until he was galloping –
   past the donkey, who shouted "Hooray!" –
   – galloping – galloping – galloping –
till he came to the gate with Dobbin leaning over it –

"Mind out!" shouted Brainbox; and Dobbin drew to one side and Brainbox JUMPED. He went sailing over the five-barred gate, into the meadow.

"I've come to live here," said Brainbox to Dobbin. "To be your friend."

"Good," said Dobbin. "Very good indeed." He kicked up his heels for joy, and so did Brainbox. Then they galloped round the meadow together. When they were tired, they settled down to standing side by side, head to tail. Brainbox swished his tail to stop the flies from settling on Dobbin's head, and Dobbin swished his tail to stop the flies from settling on Brainbox's.

The two friends lived together in their meadow, keeping each other company, for many, many years. They were happy horses.

HOW THE LITTLE BOY AND THE LITTLE GIRL WENT FOR A WALK IN THE MUD

A French fairy tale

Once upon a time there were a little boy and a little girl, and one day they decided to go for a walk. As it had just been pouring with rain, there was mud everywhere. And as there was mud everywhere, the path where the little boy and the little girl were walking was muddy too. And because the path was so very muddy, the little girl's feet suddenly slid from under her and – oops! – she fell smack into the mud on her little bottom.

The little boy then felt sorry for the little girl, so he caught hold of her with both his hands and began to pull her to her feet. As he was pulling her, his feet suddenly slid from under him and – oops! – he fell smack into the mud on his little bottom.

Then the little girl felt sorry for the little boy, so she caught hold of him with both her hands and began to pull him to his feet. As she was pulling him, her feet suddenly slid from under her and – oops! – she fell smack into the mud on her little bottom.

And so it went on:

oops! he sat smack in the mud,
oops! she sat smack in the mud,
oops! his bottom in,
oops! her bottom in,
oops! he fell,
oops! she fell,
oops! his turn,
oops! her turn,
and oops!
and oops!

And if they are still alive, they must still be in that mud, going oops!

and oops!
and oops!
and oops!

THE DONKEY THAT COULD CONQUER THE WORLD
Retold by Edward Blishen

There was once a man who had nothing in the world but the clothes he stood up in, which were also the clothes he lay down in to sleep, and a donkey. It was an old donkey, and it hadn't been well-fed. The man could hardly afford to feed himself. You could see that poor donkey's ribs. And I think if you'd sat on it, it would have fallen down.

All the same, the donkey was all the man had to sell. No one, of course, would buy it where there were fine fit donkeys to be bought. So the man decided he must go travelling until he found a country where they'd never seen a donkey. If people didn't know what a donkey ought to look like, perhaps they would buy this sad old bag of bones.

At last he came to a land where the people stared at the donkey with amazement. What sort of creature was that? They'd never seen such an animal before.

"Well, it's not one of your ordinary beasts," said the man. "It's called a donkey. It has wonderful gifts. A donkey, if it wants to, is able to conquer the whole world."

Well, one person told another about the marvellous animal. "It's called a dinkey," he said, and that person told another. "It's called a dankey," he said, and so on. And at last someone told the King of the country, and he ordered the poor man to be brought to him.

"I would like to buy this dunkey of yours," said the King.

"It's not a dunkey, it's a donkey, Your Majesty," said the poor man. "And I'm not sure that it's for sale. You see, it can conquer the world, and so is very valuable. It is possible, Your Majesty, that you couldn't afford to buy it."

The King had been anxious to buy the donkey. Now he was *very* anxious to buy it. "Name your price," he said.

"I'll sell it," said the poor man, "for its weight in gold."

The King agreed at once, and they had the donkey weighed. Though it was so bony, it was still heavy enough to make the poor man a rich man. He took his gold joyfully and left for home.

The King was delighted to have this marvellous rare beast in his stables. He gave orders that the donkey was to be well fed, and in no time that gloomy, bony creature had become a happy, chubby creature. In six months he was as round as a ball. He wasn't any longer in danger of starving to death, though some feared he might simply burst.

One day the country was attacked by the King of the country next door. His army made a great circle round the city in which the donkey, now the fattest in the world, was living so happily. But the people of the city weren't a bit afraid. Didn't their King own a creature that could conquer the world! They took the donkey from its comfortable stable and brought it out to face the enemy.

The donkey hadn't been outside his stable yard for many months. He was delighted to find himself in a large green open space, and paid no attention to the great army spread out in front of him. He did what any donkey would do. He rolled on the ground, his legs in the air, and he hee-hawed and hee-hawed to his heart's content. He'd never hee-hawed so much before.

As for the enemy, they'd never seen a donkey in their lives. They were horrified. What was this creature, round as a barrel, waving its legs and uttering a sound like a whole army of trumpets? But before they could make up their minds what to do about it, the donkey had noticed their horses. They looked to him like donkeys, and he hadn't

talked to another donkey since . . . well, he couldn't remember. He turned the right way up, got to his feet, and raced towards the enemy.

And that did it! The enemy were terrified. They leapt on their horses, turned them in the direction of their own country, and fled as fast as they could, if not faster.

And you can imagine what joy they left behind them. People danced in the street. The King ordered himself a new and more glorious crown. The donkey was led back to his stable and given an enormous meal. The main street in the city was renamed Donkey Street, and in the main square they built a great column, with a statue of the donkey at the top. And the square was renamed Heehaw Square.

As for the donkey, it got fatter – and then fatter still. But I think I would have heard if it had actually burst.

THE LORY WHO LONGED FOR HONEY

Leila Berg

Once upon a time, in a hot sunny country, lived a very bright and beautiful parrot. He was red and green and gold and blue, with a dark purple top to his head. His real name was Lory. And he lived on honey.

There were hundreds of flowers growing among the trees, so all he had to do when he was hungry was to fly down and lick the honey out of the flowers. As a matter of fact, he had a tongue that was specially shaped for getting honey out of flowers. So he always had plenty to eat, and managed very well. All day long he flew about in the sun while the monkeys chattered and the bright birds screamed. And as long as he had plenty of honey, he was perfectly happy.

Then one day a sailor came to the forest looking for parrots. He found the parrot that liked honey and took him away. He didn't know that this parrot's real name was a Lory. He didn't know that he had a tongue specially shaped for getting honey out of flowers. He didn't even know he liked honey. He only knew he was a very bright and beautiful parrot and he meant to take him to England and sell him. So on board the ship he fed the parrot on sunflower seeds and taught him to say: "What have you got, what have you got, what have you got for me?" And whenever the Lory said this, the sailor gave him a sunflower seed. Although, as a matter of fact, he would very much sooner have had honey.

When they reached England, the sailor sold the parrot who liked honey to an old lady who lived in a cottage on a hill. She didn't know much about parrots. She didn't know the parrot was a Lory. She didn't know he had a special tongue for licking honey out of flowers. She didn't even know he liked honey.

But she thought his red and green feathers, his gold and blue feathers, and the dark purple feathers on the top of his head were beautiful. She called him Polly, and fed him on bits of bread and biscuit.

Whenever he said, as he often did: "What have you got, what have you got, what have you got for me?" she would give him a bit of bread or biscuit. But, of course, he would very much sooner have had honey.

Now the old lady lived by herself and had to work very hard to make enough money to buy food. Generally she had just bread and margarine for tea, because she couldn't afford to buy honey even for herself, although she liked it.

Then one day when she wasn't in the least expecting it, the old lady's nephew who lived in South Africa sent her a present. It was a wooden box carefully packed with straw. Some of the straw was already poking between the boards, but it was impossible to tell what was inside.

When the postman brought it, he said: "Looks like a nice surprise, lady. Maybe some jam or some fruit."

She carried the box carefully into her sitting-room and unfastened it. It wasn't jam or fruit. It was six jars of honey all wrapped up in straw. Inside was a note which said:

Dear Auntie,
I have managed to get a very nice job in South Africa,

and I am making quite a bit of money. I am sure you are not able to buy all the things you need, so I am sending you six jars of honey. If you like them, I will send some more.

Love from your nephew – Robert

When she had read the letter she was tremendously excited and pleased, because it was so long since anyone had sent her a present and today it wasn't even her birthday. She took out the jars very carefully and put them in a row in the larder. Then she cleared up all the straw and paper and string, and said to herself: "I'll start the first jar at tea-time today."

When the clock struck half-past three, the old lady put the kettle on the gas, and began to cut some bread. It was certainly rather early for tea, but the old lady was so excited about the honey that she couldn't wait any longer. She put the bread and margarine on the table, took a plate and a knife, and a cup and saucer and spoon out of the cupboard, and then she went to the larder.

All this made Polly very excited. He wasn't in his cage, but on a separate perch where he could turn somersaults if he liked. The old lady let him sit here in the afternoons. He could tell it was tea-time, and when the old lady went to the larder he expected she would bring out some cake or fruit.

So he shouted at the top of his voice: "What have you got, what have you got, what have you got for me?" When the old lady brought out neither cake nor fruit, but only a jar of yellow stuff, Polly was rather puzzled. But as soon as he saw her take some on her knife and spread the sticky stuff on her bread, and eat it with such pleasure, he knew it was honey.

And as soon as he knew it was honey, he knew he absolutely must think of some way of getting it for himself.

The old lady never dreamt of giving the Lory honey. She didn't know much about parrots. She didn't know he was called a Lory. She didn't know he had a tongue specially shaped for getting honey out of flowers. She didn't even know he liked honey.

But all the time the old lady was spreading the honey on her first slice of bread and thinking how wonderfully kind her nephew was to send it, and what an unexpected treat it was, the Lory was working out a plan.

Now parrots, as you know, are very clever at remembering words and also at imitating people, and sometimes when they talk they can make their voice sound as if it is coming from a different part of the house altogether, so that you have no idea it is the parrot talking at all.

While the old lady was eating her bread and honey and enjoying it tremendously, she suddenly heard a *Miaow!* It was really the Lory, but she didn't know that.

"There's a kitten outside," she said. "Poor thing, I expect it's lost. I'll let it in so that it can get warm by the fire." And she went to the door and opened it.

Polly just had time to flutter on to the table and take a mouthful of honey with his special tongue and get on his perch again before she came back.

"How very strange," she said, "I'm sure I heard a kitten. Yet I've looked in the street, and there isn't a kitten to be seen."

Polly winked and shouted: "What have you got, what have you got, what have you got for me?" But the old lady still didn't know he was after the honey.

While the lady was spreading her *second* slice of bread, he

thought of another plan. This time he made a noise like the
kettle boiling over.

"Goodness!" cried the old lady, jumping up. "That will
put the stove out, unless I hurry."

And while she rushed out into the kitchen, Polly flew
down and took his second big mouthful of honey.

"That's very peculiar," said the old lady, coming back
again just as Polly scrambled on to his perch. "The kettle's
perfectly all right, and not boiling over at all." But she still
didn't understand the Lory was after her honey.

Then he had what he thought was his best plan of all. He
made a noise like big drops of rain falling on the roof.

"Oh heavens!" said the poor old lady. "Now I shall have
to bring all the washing in."

79

And she left her tea with the pot of honey standing on the table, and went outside to fetch in the washing before it got soaked.

She was a long time, because she had washed a tablecloth, two sheets, a pillow-slip, a towel, a frock, a cardigan and the curtains from the sitting-room. And while she was taking them all off the line, the Lory was swallowing honey as fast as he could.

At last, her arms full of washing, the old lady came back into the room. "That's funny," she said, as she looked at the window. "The sun is shining as brightly as ever. I do believe I've brought all the washing in for nothing."

"And that's funnier still!" she went on with a little scream, looking at the table. "I do believe someone's been eating my honey!"

She picked up the jar and looked at it. There was just a scraping left at the bottom. Yet she had only opened the jar a few minutes ago.

"It must be a burglar," she said, and feeling very brave she began to look under the furniture and inside the cupboards and wherever a burglar might find space to hide.

All the time she was hunting, the Lory was turning somersaults on his perch and shrieking at the top of his voice: "What have you got, what have you got, what have you got for me?" He felt very pleased with himself, and he didn't care a bit that he had made the old lady go to all the trouble of bringing in her washing, and on top of that had eaten almost the whole of a jar of honey that her nephew had sent from South Africa.

When the old lady had decided there was no burglar in the house, she went back to the tea-table. And then she noticed drips of honey leading over the table cloth, over the floor, and up to Polly's perch. She reached up and touched his perch, and, sure enough, that was sticky too.

"Why, you rascal!" she said. "I do believe it was you who stole the honey."

And that was how the old lady who didn't know much about parrots discovered that Lories like honey better than anything else in the world. After that, she always gave her Lory some honey for his tea, and she managed it quite well because her nephew in South Africa sent her six jars every month.

But do you know, she never found out it was the Lory who played those tricks on her just to get a taste of her honey!

81

BRER RABBIT, HE'S A GOOD FISHERMAN

Joel Chandler Harris

One day, when Brer Rabbit, and Brer Fox, and Brer Bear and a whole lot of them was clearing a new ground for to plant a roasting-pear patch, the sun began to get sort of hot, and Brer Rabbit, he got tired; but he didn't let on, 'cause he feared the others would call him lazy, and he keep on carrying away rubbish and piling it up, till by and by he holler out that he got a thorn in his hand, and then he take and slip off, and hunt for a cool place for to rest. After a while he come across a well with a bucket hanging in it.

"That looks cool," says Brer Rabbit, says he. "And cool I 'specs she is. I'll just about get in there and take a nap," and with that, in he jump, he did, and he ain't no sooner fix himself than the bucket begin to go down. Brer Rabbit, he was mighty scared. He know where he come from, but he don't know where he's going. Suddenly he feel the bucket hit the water, and there she sat, but Brer Rabbit, he keep mighty still, 'cause he don't know what minute's going to be the next. He just lay there and shook and shiver.

Brer Fox always got one eye on Brer Rabbit, and when he slip off from the new ground, Brer Fox, he sneak after him. He knew Brer Rabbit was after some project or another, and he took and crope off, he did, and watch him. Brer Fox see Brer Rabbit come to the top of the well and stop, and then he see him jump in the bucket, and then, lo and behold! he see him go down out of sight. Brer Fox was the most 'stonished fox that you ever laid eyes on. He sat down in the bushes and thought and thought, but he don't make no head nor tails of this kind of business. Then he say to himself, says he,

"Well, if this don't beat everything!" says he. "Right down there in that well Brer Rabbit keep his money hid, and if it ain't that, he done gone and 'scovered a gold mine, and if it ain't that, then I'm a-going to see what's in there."

Brer Fox crope up a little nearer, he did, and listen, but he don't hear no fuss, and he keep on getting nearer, and yet he don't hear nothing. By and by he get up close and peep down, but he don't see nothing, and he don't hear nothing. All this time Brer Rabbit was mighty near scared out of his skin, and he feared for to move 'cause the bucket might keel over and spill him in the water. While he was saying his prayers over and over, Brer Fox holler out,

"Heyo, Brer Rabbit! Who you visitin' down there?" says he.

"Who? Me? Oh, I'm just a-fishing, Brer Fox," says Brer Rabbit, says he. "I just say to myself that I'd sort of s'prise you all with a mess of fishes, and so here I is, and there's the fishes. I'm a-fishing for supper, Brer Fox," says Brer Rabbit, says he.

"Is there many of them down there, Brer Rabbit?" says Brer Fox, says he.

"Lots of them, Brer Fox, scores and scores of them. The water is naturally alive with them. Come down and help me haul them in, Brer Fox," says Brer Rabbit, says he.

"How I going to get down, Brer Rabbit?"

"Jump in the other bucket, Brer Fox. I'll fetch you down all safe and sound."

Brer Rabbit talked so happy and so sweet that Brer Fox he jump in the bucket, he did, and so he went down, 'cause his weight pulled Brer Rabbit up. When they pass one another on the half-way ground, Brer Rabbit he sing out:

> "Good-bye, Brer Fox, take care o' your clothes,
> For this is the way the world goes;
> Some goes up and some goes down,
> You'll get to the bottom all safe and soun'."

When Brer Rabbit got out, he gallop off and told the folks what the well belonged to, that Brer Fox was down there muddying up the drinking water, and then he gallop back to the well, and holler down to Brer Fox:

> "Here come a man with a great big gun –
> When he haul you up, you jump and run."

Well, soon enough Brer Fox was out of the well, and in just about half an hour both of them was back on the new ground working just as if they'd never heard of no well. But every now and then Brer Rabbit would burst out laughing, and old Brer Fox would scowl and say nothing.

TEENY–TINY

Joseph Jacobs

Once upon a time there was a teeny-tiny woman who lived in a teeny-tiny house in a teeny-tiny village. Now, one day this teeny-tiny woman put on her teeny-tiny bonnet, and went out of her teeny-tiny house to take a teeny-tiny walk. And when this teeny-tiny woman had gone a teeny-tiny way, she came to a teeny-tiny gate; so the teeny-tiny woman opened the teeny-tiny gate, and went into a teeny-tiny churchyard. And when this teeny-tiny woman had got into the teeny-tiny churchyard, she saw a teeny-tiny bone on a teeny-tiny grave, and the teeny-tiny woman said to her teeny-tiny self, "This teeny-tiny bone will make me some teeny-tiny soup for my teeny-tiny supper." So the teeny-tiny woman put the teeny-tiny bone into her teeny-tiny pocket, and went home to her teeny-tiny house.

Now, when the teeny-tiny woman got home to her teeny-tiny house, she was a teeny-tiny bit tired; so she went up her teeny-tiny stairs to her teeny-tiny bed, and put the teeny-tiny bone into a teeny-tiny cupboard. And when this teeny-tiny woman had been to sleep a teeny-tiny time, she was awakened by a teeny-tiny voice from the teeny-tiny cupboard, which said:

"Give me my bone!"

The teeny-tiny woman was a teeny-tiny bit frightened, so she hid her teeny-tiny head under the teeny-tiny clothes and went to sleep again. And when she had been to sleep again a teeny-tiny time, the teeny-tiny voice again cried out from the teeny-tiny cupboard a teeny-tiny louder:

"Give me my bone!"

This made the teeny-tiny woman a teeny-tiny bit more frightened, so she hid her teeny-tiny head a teeny-tiny further under the teeny-tiny clothes. And when the teeny-tiny woman had been to sleep again a teeny-tiny time, the teeny-tiny voice from the teeny-tiny cupboard said again a teeny-tiny louder:

"Give me my bone!"

And this teeny-tiny woman was a teeny-tiny bit more frightened, but she put her teeny-tiny head out of the teeny-tiny clothes, and said in her loudest teeny-tiny voice, "TAKE IT!"

THE PRINCE WHO HAD DONKEY'S EARS

Retold by Edward Blishen

Once there were a king and a queen and their newborn baby son. He was a prince, of course. And there were three fairies, who'd come with gifts for the baby.

The first fairy smiled beautifully and said: "No prince in the whole world will be more handsome!"

And the second fairy smiled even more beautifully and said: "No prince in the whole world will be wiser or more honest."

The third fairy smiled only a very small smile. She was worried. The handsomest prince in the world! The wisest prince in the world! The most honest prince in the world! Wouldn't that make him the proudest prince in the world? Wouldn't he grow up thinking there was no one like him? Wouldn't he grow up too proud by half?

She thought, and she thought, and then she said: "My gift is that he shall have . . . donkey's ears. Very big, very pointed, very hairy donkey's ears. And that will prevent him from being too proud."

You can imagine how anxious the king and queen were. They watched the young prince grow more and more handsome. They watched him grow more and more wise, and more and more honest. But they also watched his ears grow huger and huger, and hairier and hairier, and more and more pointed. No doubt about it, those were donkey's ears!

Well, they didn't want anyone to know about *that*. So they let his hair grow. It grew to his shoulders, and no one would have known that he had ears at all. But then it went on growing. The time came when the prince's hair simply had to be trimmed.

But the barber who cut his hair was sure to find out about those dreadful ears! What was to be done?

What the king and queen did was to send for the best barber in the land. He was to trim the prince's hair, they said, once a week. He would be wonderfully well paid for it. But in doing it he would discover . . . something rather surprising. And about that he must say nothing. If he told anyone at all what he had seen, he would be punished with death.

The barber wondered what he would find under the prince's hair. But of course he couldn't say no to the king

and queen. And for a barber it was the best job in the kingdom. Even the king didn't have a barber who lived in the palace, was paid in gold, and ate royal food at the royal table. The barber was happy.

That's to say, he was happy until he trimmed the prince's hair for the first time. Then, at once, he found those terrible ears. He was so shocked that he dropped his scissors. The prince said sadly:

"I know you have promised the king and queen that you will keep this secret to yourself." And the barber nodded and picked up his scissors and went on trimming the prince's hair.

But oh, that secret! It is a terrible thing to have such a secret to keep. The barber longed to tell someone else, anyone at all. He didn't want people to laugh at the prince. He just wanted to share the secret. Well, you know how having a secret makes you long to give it away.

So the barber was well paid and well fed but he was unhappy. And then he remembered that living in a forest near the palace was an old man known to be extremely wise. So the barber slipped out and visited him. He didn't tell the wise man what the secret was. He simply said he had one, an awful one, and longed to tell it. What could he do?

Well, said the wise man, there *was* an answer to that. The barber should find some place as lonely as possible. There he should dig a hole. Then he should tell his secret to the hole, and fill it in again.

"The ground," said the wise man, "will never give you away. You will have told your secret and only the earth will know of it."

So that's what the barber did. He went to the loneliest place he knew, he dug a hole, and he told his secret to the hole. And my goodness, how cheerful he suddenly felt! He filled the hole in again, and he sang all the way back to the palace. That surely was the end of his troubles!

But it wasn't.

Out of the earth where the barber had dug his hole, some stout reeds grew. Now, they were just the sort of reeds for making whistles. Along came two shepherds, cut two reeds, and made two whistles. And then they played them.

But these weren't at all like ordinary whistles. They didn't play the tunes the shepherds wanted to play. Instead, out of both came a thin whistling voice that sang, again and again:

> "The prince has donkey's ears,
> Did you know?
> The prince has donkey's ears . . .
> Did you know?"

Well, soon everyone knew. The shepherds told their friends, and their friends told *their* friends, and from friend to friend it passed until the king heard of it. He had the shepherds brought to him, and ordered them to play. Oh, they tried so hard to make the whistles play some other tune! But all that came out from both, in that thin whistling voice, was the song that now the whole kingdom knew:

> "The prince has donkey's ears,
> Did you know?
> The prince has donkey's ears . . .
> Did you know?"

Imagine the king's anger! He knew who must have given the secret away. It could only be the barber. He ordered the poor man to be brought to him at once. He had been warned! If he told anyone about the prince's ears, he would die. And the king called for the executioner.

But at that moment the prince stepped forward.

"Father, *father!*" he cried. "Why should the barber be punished for telling the truth? It is true, I *have* donkey's ears! But what does the shape of my ears matter? I'd rather have ordinary ears, of course. But, I suppose, if they're good enough for an honest donkey, they're good enough for an honest prince."

And with his hands he swept his hair back so everyone could see his ears. And they all gasped.

They gasped and they turned pale. And then they began to cheer.

"But," they cried, "your ears are just like anybody else's!"

And so they were. Because there had been a part of the fairy's gift that she had kept to herself. It was that if ever the prince showed that he wasn't proud, that there was no danger of his being the proudest prince in the world, then his ears would become ordinary ears.

And so everybody was happy. I think you can guess who was the happiest of all. It was the barber, of course. If the prince hadn't lost his donkey's ears, the barber would have lost his barber's head.

But what about the whistles, you ask? Well, there was a naughty child or two who tried them out, in the hope of hearing that thin whistling voice crying:

> The prince has donkey's ears,
> Did you know?

But now that everyone knew, and anyway the prince had ears like anyone else, the song was never heard again.

THE ENORMOUS
APPLE PIE

Diana Ross

Miss Pussy is cooking a pie, an enormous apple pie. This afternoon all her nieces and nephews are coming to tea, and just imagine how many she has, twenty nephews and nieces; for she comes of a big family and all are married and have children save Miss Pussy herself, which is a pity, for Miss Pussy is good and kind and would make an excellent wife and mother.

So now you can reckon, with so many to eat it, what a very big pie Miss Pussy is to make.

At her side are two great baskets full of golden apples, Bramley Seedlings every one, freshly picked this morning and not a single windfall among them. On the shelf is a tall red canister full of demerara sugar, and her spice box is open on the table scenting the whole kitchen with the sweet smell of nutmeg, clove, cinnamon and allspice, bay leaves, ginger and mace.

First of all Miss Pussy peels and cores the apples with the silver knife her uncle left her, and she throws the first peel over her left shoulder to see who her lover will be; and it falls in the shape of an O, and she smiles to herself at her folly, and anyway, she does not know anyone with a name beginning with O.

Then the apples are sliced up fine into the enormous basin in which she will bake them. She has put a quart jug in the centre to hold up the piecrust, and when the dish is nearly filled to the brim she sprinkles in the sugar, spoonful after spoonful, pours in enough water to keep it all moist, stirs in cloves, cinnamon and a scattering of almonds, and there is the pie all ready to be covered.

So now she must prepare the pastry, and she goes to the cupboard and pulls out the flour bin, sets her shining copper scales on the table and weighs out the flour, six pounds of it. She pours it into the great bowl she must use for the mixing, and then weighs out the lard, a full three pounds. She mixes this into the flour, sifting it and rubbing it till it is so finely mixed there is not a lump anywhere, a pinch of baking powder, a good squeeze of lemon juice, and then she pours in the water while mixing it all together with a strong wooden spoon; and let me tell you this is hard work, as you may find if you should try. So when the dough is thoroughly mixed Miss Pussy puts on the kettle and sits down for a rest and a nice cup of tea. And when she is rested she sets about rolling out the dough. She sprinkles flour all over the kitchen table, for her pastry board would be far too small for the cover of this pie, and she takes her best glass rolling pin painted with schooners and lovers' knots which Old Tom Cat once gave her after his time at sea in a whaler, and she rolls out the dough till it is even and thin all over the table, then carefully, carefully, so as not to break it, she lifts it on to the top of her pie dish, trims all round it with a pair of scissors, moistens the edge of the dish and the edge of the pastry, presses the two together, and twists all the odd pieces into a twirly decoration to finish it off, with a pastry rose in the centre. She remembers to prick little holes in the pastry here and there in a pattern to let the steam out, and then she opens the oven, which she lit early this morning, and she finds it just right, not too hot and not too cold. So in she puts her pie and shuts the door, and sets about cleaning up the kitchen.

This done, she has all the other preparations to make, so she busies herself about the house, making it all neat and tidy, and she does not rest until half-past one, and now the pie should be done. So now she opens the oven door and oh! what a lovely smell of scented apple and crisp brown piecrust. Miss Pussy lifts out the pie and puts it on a table by the window, for on this warm autumn day she thinks it will be nice to eat it cold with junket and a gallon of cream.

Now that every single thing is in order, the house clean, the table set, the sandwiches cut, the cakes and buns she has been making for a week past all set out on her best Coalport dishes, Miss Pussy thinks she will sleep till her guests arrive, for then she will be fresh to entertain them. So Miss Pussy goes up to her bedroom and leaves her wonderful pie cooling beside the open window.

Oh! Miss Pussy, will you never learn caution? Will you never remember all the rascally people in the world?

No sooner is Miss Pussy asleep than who should come slouching along the road but old Jackanapes and Snatch, his friend, gossiping of this and that and ready for any kind of mischief.

Snatch is the first to smell the sweet smell of spiced apples, and nudging Jackanapes he points at the kitchen window framing the pie and then at the window above with the curtains drawn, and no words need to pass between them. In a moment the two are in the garden and climbing in at the open window.

"Let us not cut the piecrust," whispers Jackanapes, "for we may have a fine joke as well as a good feast."

97

So very carefully they prise round the edge of the piecrust with a knife till they can lift it off and lay it to one side. And then with all haste they eat up the apples. Think of it, only think of it! Those two rascals alone eat up all the fruit that was to have fed twenty nephews and nieces, to say nothing of Miss Pussy herself; every single bit and the last drop of juice lapped up, and Jackanapes rudely spits the cloves out all over the floor.

Miss Pussy, Miss Pussy, why do you sleep so sound?

This done, Jackanapes whispers to Snatch, and away they skip as fast as they can, and with stomachs so full it is a marvel they can move so nimbly. Down to the marshes they go, and gather as many great croaking frogs as they can find, and they tie them up in their handkerchiefs, and gathering handfuls of moss they run back to Miss Pussy's.

Miss Pussy's blind is still fast drawn so into the kitchen they go. They lay the moss on the bottom of the dish, and then they lift on the piecrust. Then they take the frogs one by one, and raising the crust just a little they slip the frogs inside it and shut it down again, until every frog is inside, jumping about on the moss and trying to get out. Jackanapes quickly makes up a paste of flour and water, and fixes down the piecrust to the dish, then he and Snatch run off, leaving the pie by the window just as they had found it.

At half-past three Miss Pussy wakes up, and dresses herself with care, little thinking what has gone on below while she has slept.

No sooner is she dressed than a carriage rolls up, and out jump her nephews and nieces, all twenty of them, laughing and talking, and hungry for their tea.

"Come in, my dears," says Miss Pussy. "Today I will not keep you waiting, we will eat our tea at once, for I have a huge surprise for you. Yes, I may say a very big surprise," for Miss Pussy is justly proud of her enormous apple pie.

The nephews and nieces are making such a noise with their chatter that when Miss Pussy goes to bring in the pie she does not hear the croaking that comes from it.

When they see it what a shout comes from her guests, what cries of, "Oh, Aunt Pussy, however did you do it?" and, "Oh, Aunt Pussy, I could eat it all up myself."

And there is so much innocent excitement that no one notices how Jackanapes and Snatch have sidled up to the window and are peeping in to enjoy the consternation they have so unkindly planned.

Miss Pussy takes up the knife and fork.

"Now I will cut the enormous pie," she says, "and the very first piece shall go to the quietest."

At once there is a hush with subdued laughter and whispers from all the nephews and nieces, and now that it is quiet, why, whatever is this?

CROAK CROAK CROAAAK CROAK.

The nieces and nephews all look at each other. Miss Pussy frowns, for she thinks that one of the children is doing it to tease her.

CROAK CROAK CROAK CROAAAK CROAK.

And this time it unmistakably comes from inside the pie. Miss Pussy is astonished. She cannot think what it can be. So she quickly thrusts the knife through the crust and cuts out a large slice.

The great slippery frogs come leaping out in a body, croak-croak-croaking, their golden eyes shining.

Miss Pussy bursts into tears. The nieces shriek. The nephews laugh. "Oh! Aunt Pussy, indeed and indeed this is a great surprise!" For they think it an excellent joke, the humour of small boys being what it is.

But if Jackanapes and Snatch take pleasure from the distress of Miss Pussy, it is not for long.

For now that the frogs are all out of the pie they gather themselves in order around the largest among them, and he, with a great air, draws a fiddle from under his arm, and each of the others produces a musical instrument, till there is a complete orchestra of flutes and strings, and bowing to Miss Pussy, who is dumb with amazement, they strike up a pleasant tune. Motioning to Miss Pussy that she shall follow them, they lead the way back into the pie.

What! Follow a band of frogs into an apple pie! Why, the thing is impossible! But as Miss Pussy and her nieces and nephews crowd round to peer into the pie the opening seems to widen, and quite easily they find themselves walking in a mossy glade, so delightful and charming they think they have found the way to paradise.

The place is enclosed by a semicircle of rocks covered over with moss and ferns, with brilliant flowers growing in among them. A waterfall pours over the highest point into a deep clear pool, from which flows a shallow stream, running over fine sand and pretty coloured stones, and bordered with forget-me-nots and irises.

A willow tree hangs over the farther side in which a willow wren is sitting, singing its song, and though its voice is small and shrill it is distinctly heard above the sound of falling water and the music the frogs are making. For these now are ranged on a ledge of rock, settled down ready to play their music for the rest of the afternoon.

Now Miss Pussy sees that a cloth is laid out on the grassy lawn, and on it a feast is spread. And what a feast. Why, even Miss Pussy, for all her generosity and culinary skill, could never have made such a feast as this.

There are nine-and-twenty dishes of sandwiches, egg and cress, cucumber, savoury, and sweet. There are seventeen honeycombs and six big jars of strawberry jam. There are prawns piled high on dishes decorated with seaweed, fresh crab and lobster and sardines served up in cockle shells.

There are thirty-nine blancmanges, pink and white, and forty jellies of every pretty colour imaginable. There are twenty-five iced cakes each as big as a wedding cake, and forty plates of smaller ones. As for all the dishes of sweets and ice-creams, even if I could tell you all the different kinds there are, you might be tired of hearing it.

And standing in the shallow water in the shadow of a rock to keep them cool are crystal decanters of lemonade, ginger beer, raspberry cordial, cider and cowslip wine.

Since the feast is obviously meant for them, and since the wonders and excitement have done nothing to reduce their appetite, the nephews and nieces quickly range themselves about the cloth and wait for Miss Pussy to bid them to begin. When they do they eat and eat and eat, and stint themselves in nothing, but still at the end of it there is so much left that you would think yourself lucky to get the hundredth part of it.

So now they get up and the cloth is cleared away, but they do not see by whom; and then the nieces and nephews scatter about the lovely place, some dancing minuets to the music the frogs are making, others playing games, or climbing among the rocks, others paddling or gathering bunches of flowers to give to Miss Pussy; and she is in a perfect dream of delight sitting in the warm sunshine watching her nieces and nephews enjoying themselves.

But now the willow wren falls silent, a soft mist begins to

drift about the glade. The frogs are playing quiet music, and a nightingale is heard.

"Come, children," calls Miss Pussy. "It is getting late. You must finish your games. We must be getting home."

"Oh, Aunt Pussy," cry the nephews and nieces, "must we go so soon? I have never been in such a place before. I should like to stay here for ever."

"Oh! Aunt Pussy, however did you contrive such a wonderful outing?"

But this Miss Pussy cannot answer, for she herself does not know how it happened.

At last she has got them all together, and then the frogs escort them up a little winding path which leads out of the glade; and without quite noticing how it happens Miss Pussy finds herself standing in her little room, her nieces and nephews all around her just as they were when they first peered into the pie.

So is it all a dream? Miss Pussy might almost think so, except that one of her nieces is still wearing a wreath in her hair which she wove by the banks of the stream, and not one of the flowers it is made of is out in Miss Pussy's garden at this time of the year.

So then Miss Pussy bustles about, dressing the nephews and nieces and wrapping them up for their journey home, for though it was hot enough this afternoon when they came, now it is dark there is a little bite in the air.

Next day comes old Jackanapes.

"Oh, Miss Pussy," he says, "it is noised about in the village that you were taken to an enchanted glade, and there had such a feast as was never heard of before."

Miss Pussy is very pleased to talk of her wonderful outing, and tells old Jackanapes all about it.

"Since you were feasted in the glade," says he, "I suppose all the good things you had prepared yourself are still in the house and still to be eaten?" This is really what he has come for, since he thinks he may get a share in the good things.

But there you are wrong, Mr Jackanapes, and a good thing, too, since you deserve so badly, for Miss Pussy was up early today and packed up all her good things and carried them over to the orphanage, so that others should benefit from the good fortune she has had.

When Jackanapes learns this he will waste his time no longer, but suddenly goes off, and Miss Pussy innocently wonders what has put him out of humour.

THE CAT AND THE MOUSE
James Reeves

The cat and the mouse played in the malthouse. The cat bit the mouse's tail off. "Pray, puss, give me my tail."

"No," says the cat, "I'll not give you your tail, till you go to the cow, and fetch me some milk."

First she leaped and then she ran, till she came to the cow, and thus began:

"Pray, Cow, give me milk, that I may give cat milk, that cat may give me my own tail again."

"No," says the cow, "I will give you no milk, till you go to the farmer and get me some hay."

First she leaped, and then she ran, till she came to the farmer, and thus began:

"Pray, Farmer, give me hay, that I may give cow hay, that cow may give me milk, that I may give cat milk, that cat may give me my own tail again."

"No," says the farmer, "I'll give you no hay, till you go to the butcher and fetch me some meat."

First she leaped, and then she ran, till she came to the butcher, and thus began:

"Pray, Butcher, give me meat, that I may give farmer meat, that farmer may give me hay, that I may give cow hay, that cow may give me milk, that I may give cat milk, that cat may give me my own tail again."

"No," says the butcher, "I'll give you no meat, till you go to the baker and fetch me some bread."

First she leaped, and then she ran, till she came to the baker, and thus began:

"Pray, Baker, give me bread, that I may give butcher bread, that butcher may give me meat, that I may give farmer meat, that farmer may give me hay, that I may give cow hay, that cow may give me milk, that I may give cat milk, that cat may give me my own tail again."

"Yes," says the baker, "I'll give you some bread, but if you eat my meal, I'll cut off your head."

Then the baker gave mouse bread, and mouse gave butcher bread, and butcher gave mouse meat, and mouse gave farmer meat, and farmer gave mouse hay, and mouse gave cow hay, and cow gave mouse milk, and mouse gave cat milk, and cat gave mouse her own tail again!

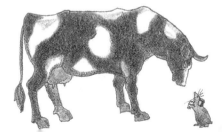

THE LITTLE BOY
WHO DIDN'T ALWAYS
TELL THE TRUTH

A traditional French tale

There was once a farmer who lived in a village in France. He had a small son who told the truth some of the time; but some of the time, he didn't.

One day the farmer sent the boy to look after the sheep. He was to drive them to the top of a hill outside the village, where the grass grew long and sweet.

Hardly had the boy gone than he was back again, quite out of breath. He said, "Father! father! Get your gun! I saw a hare on the hill, as big as a horse!"

"A hare as big as a horse?" said his father. "I can't imagine that!"

"Well, perhaps it wasn't quite as big as a grown-up horse," said the boy. "But it was as big as a horse six weeks old."

"A hare as big as a horse six weeks old," said his father. "I can't imagine that!"

"Well, perhaps it wasn't quite as big as a horse six weeks old. But it was as big as a calf."

"A hare as big as a calf? I can't imagine that!"

"Well, perhaps it wasn't quite as big as a calf. But it was as big as a sheep."

"A hare as big as a sheep? I can't imagine that."

"Well, perhaps it wasn't quite as big as a sheep. But it was as big as a lamb."

"A hare as big as a lamb? I can't imagine that!"

"Well, perhaps it wasn't quite as big as a lamb. But it was as big as a cat."

"A hare as big as a cat? I can't imagine that."

"Well, perhaps it wasn't quite as big as a cat. But it was as big as a rat."

"A hare as big as a rat? I can't imagine that!"

"Well, perhaps it wasn't quite as big as a rat. But it was as big as a mouse."

"A hare as big as a mouse? I can't imagine that."

"Well, perhaps it wasn't quite as big as a mouse. But it was as big as a fly."

"A hare as big as a fly? Oh, my son! I don't think you saw anything at all!"

And he sent the little storyteller back to look after the sheep.

PRICKETY PRACKETY

Diana Ross

There was once a hen called Prickety Prackety. She was a little golden brown bantam hen, and she walked about the garden on the tips of her toes – and she pecked here and pecked there and was busy and gay the whole day long.

And once a day she felt like laying an egg.

Away she went to the hen-house: "Cluck, Cluck, Cluck!" And she'd climb into the nesting box and fluff herself out and make gentle noises in her throat as soft as her own pretty feathers, and she'd sit, and she'd blink her eyes and go into a dozy-cosy and then: "Cluck, Cluck, Cluck-a-Cluck-a-Cluck!"

What a surprise! What joy! An egg! A pretty brown speckledy egg! Away she would go, not a thought in her head, peck here, peck there, on the tips of her toes.

And Anne would come at tea-time to collect the eggs, and when she saw the brown egg she would say:

"Oh! You good Mrs Prickety Prackety, you good little hen." Because Prickety Prackety was the only hen to lay brown eggs, so Anne knew that it was hers. And she would throw her out an extra handful of corn. One good turn deserves another.

But one day Prickety Prackety felt different. She felt like laying an egg. Oh, yes! But somehow not in the hen-house. So away she went by herself.

"Where are you going to, Prickety Prackety?" called Chanticleer the golden cock.

"I am going to mind my own business," she said and tossed her head. Chanticleer ran and gave her a little peck, not a hard peck, but enough of a peck to show that although he loved her dearly he wouldn't let her answer him so rudely.

But Prickety Prackety paid no attention to him. She fluttered her feathers and cried "Cloak!" because she knew he would expect it, and then she ran away, her head in the air.

"Prickety Prackety, where are you going?"

It was good sister Partlet, the old black hen, wanting her to share a dustbath near the cinder-pit.

"I am going to mind my own business," said Prickety Prackety nodding pleasantly to Partlet, and Partlet ruffled the dust in her feathers and smiled to herself.

Prickety Prackety left the garden and came to the orchard. The grass was very green underneath the apple trees and the blossom was just coming out.

"Prickety Prackety, where are you going?" cried the white ducks rootling in the grass.

"I am going to mind my own business," she said.

Beside the privet hedge was an old rusty drum.

It had been used last year to cover up the rhubarb, but now it was lying on its side and a jungle of nettles had grown up all round it.

And Prickety Prackety crept through the jungle of nettles, into the oil drum and clucked contentedly to find a few wisps of straw and dried grass. The geese and ducks smiled at each other and went on nibbling the grass in the orchard.

"Prickety Prackety has stolen a nest. I wonder if they will find it?" they thought to themselves.

Every day for twelve days Prickety Prackety disappeared into the oil drum.

Every day Chanticleer said, "Prickety Prackety, where are you going?"

Every day Partlet said, "Prickety Prackety, where are you going?"

Every day the geese and ducks said, "Prickety Prackety, where are you going?"

And every day Prickety Prackety gave the same answer with a toss of her head: "I am going to mind my own business."

And every day at tea-time Anne would come in shaking her head.

"No eggs from Prickety Prackety. She's gone right off. And just when she was doing so well too."

But worse was to come.

On the thirteenth day Prickety Prackety took a long drink and ate as much as she could when Anne put out the hot mash. And then she walked away looking *very* important.

"Where are you going, Prickety Prackety?" said Chanticleer.

"Where are you going, Prickety Prackety?" said Partlet.

"Where are you going, Prickety Prackety?" said the white ducks.

"Where are you going to, Prickety Prackety?" said the geese, following after her as if she were a procession.

But Prickety Prackety didn't even answer. She pranced along, her eyes shining.

That evening Anne came into the kitchen and said:

"Now I know why Prickety Prackety seemed to go off laying. She has stolen a nest. I shall have to go and find it."

So next day after she had put out the chicken food Anne began to look for Prickety Prackety.

She looked in the shrubbery. She looked in the vegetable garden. She looked in the sheds and outhouses. She looked along the hedges, looked in the orchard, but she didn't see Prickety Prackety, although Prickety Prackety saw her.

And every morning when it was first light and the other hens were still asleep shut up in the hen-house, Prickety Prackety would creep out of her jungle of nettles.

"Where are you going to, Prickety Prackety?" asked the little wild birds, the sparrows and finches, the blackbirds and the thrushes. But Prickety Prackety seemed not to hear, but would peck here and there, gorging herself on grubs and grass and any remains of chicken food overlooked by the others. She would drink and drink from the bowl of water by the back door, and as she lifted her head the rising sun would shine into her eyes, and then back she would go through her jungle of nettles into the oil drum, and not the least glimpse of her to be seen when the rest of the world were about.

A week went by, and another, and the blossom on the apple trees was falling so that when the soft wind blew it looked like drifting snow. And still Prickety Prackety hid in her nest.

"Have you seen Prickety Prackety?" said Chanticleer to Partlet.

"Oh! She's around somewhere," said Partlet, flaunting her feathers.

"Have you seen Prickety Prackety?" said Partlet to the ducks.

"Oh! I expect she's around somewhere," they said.

"Have you seen Prickety Prackety?" asked the ducks of the geese.

"We mind our own businesssssss," hissed the geese.

And Anne, in the kitchen yard, said: "Now, let me see. It's gone all of two weeks since Prickety Prackety stole her nest. She ought to be out come Friday. I wonder how many will hatch?"

On Friday when the sun rose the sky was quiet and clear.

Prickety Prackety crept out into the orchard shaking the dew from the nettles as she passed, so she looked like a golden hen set with diamonds.

She pecked and pranced and pecked and drank, and cocked her eye at the sun, and then she went back to her eggs, her twelve brown eggs lying on the straw in the cool green shadow of the oil drum and nettles.

She stood, her head on one side, and listened.

Tap-tap, and the smooth round surface of the nearest egg was broken and a tiny jag of shell moved and was still.

"Cluck, Cluck, Cluck, Cluck!" crooned Prickety Prackety, deep in her throat and, very satisfied, she settled on her eggs.

That evening Anne went out at tea-time.

"Coop, Coop, Coop!" she cried, the corn measure in her hand, and from every side the hens came running.

"Coop, Coop, Coop!" cried Anne.

Then who should creep out of the nettles but Prickety Prackety. "Cluck, Cluck, Cluck," she said. And out of the nettles crept, one, two, three, four, five, six, seven, eight, nine, ten, eleven, twelve little tiny, tiny chicks, so small, so tiny, so quick, so golden, so yellow – Oh, what a pretty sight!

"Well, you got them at last, Prickety Prackety," said the geese.

"And very nice too," said the ducks.

And Prickety Prackety led her family out of the orchard towards the yard. "Coop, Coop, Coop, Coop," cried Anne, scattering the corn.

But then she saw Prickety Prackety tripping towards her with one, two, three, four, five, six, seven, eight, nine, ten, eleven, twelve – yes, with twelve – tiny chicks, like little yellow clouds all about her:

"Oh!" she cried, and ran to the house.

"Caroline, Johnny, William, come quick. Prickety Prackety has hatched her chicks."

And everyone came running.

"Oh! Prickety Prackety, you *good* little hen!" And how they scattered the corn for her. But Anne was busy getting ready the special coop they kept for hens who had chicks; and they called it the Nursery Coop, for here the chicks would be safe from the cats and dogs and crows.

Very gently they lifted Prickety Prackety, and all the chicks came running as she cried to them; "Cluck, Cluck, Cluck!"

"I reckon you don't run that fast when your Mum calls you," said Anne – and the children laughed. And they all helped to carry the coop into the orchard, where the trees would shade it. And when at last Anne and the children were gone Partlet came busily by.

"A lot of trouble, but worth it. They're a fine lot, Prickety Prackety." And she nodded her head with approval.

And as for Chanticleer, he came stalking up glowing in the evening sun, and stood high on his toes, head cocked, looking at Prickety Prackety and the tiny heads poking in and out of her feathers. And then:

"Cock-a-Dooooooodle Dooooooooooo. Just look at my good wife, Prickety Prackety, and all our sons and daughters. Cock-a-Dooooooodle Doooooooo."

It was like a fanfare of trumpets.

And Prickety Prackety blinked her eyes and smiled.

HARE AND CROCODILE

A tale from Uganda

One day, Hare went to visit his sister. She'd married Crocodile, and they lived on an island in the middle of a lake, with all the other crocodiles. There were Aunt Crocodiles, many of them, and Uncle Crocodiles, many of them, and crowds of Grandfather Crocodiles, and Grandmother Crocodiles. And there were crocodiles who were everybody else's nephews and nieces. Everywhere you looked there were crocodiles. Hare wouldn't have dreamed of going there if his sister hadn't married Crocodile. But she had, and so Hare felt perfectly safe.

And he *was* safe. They gave him a very good time. And all might have been well, except for one thing. Hare loved eating eggs. And one day he saw Crocodile putting his wife's eggs into the granary. That was where they kept the grain, and other things to eat. But in one corner of the granary, as Hare couldn't help noticing, Crocodile stored all those eggs. And Hare's mouth watered!

The next day Crocodile and his wife went swimming, and Hare stayed at home. He said he had a headache and just wanted to rest, quietly. The moment they'd gone he hurried to the granary and found the eggs. They were big and yellow and delicious. He ate as many as he could and then collected the shells and buried them. He took care to wipe his mouth, then waited for his sister and Crocodile.

Oh, he said when they arrived, he was very hungry. So his sister cooked some food for him; but when it was brought, Hare found he could eat nothing. His stomach was full of egg. He went to bed early, and by the morning he felt much better. Again his sister and Crocodile went swimming. Again Hare stayed at home, saying he needed to rest. And again, I'm afraid, he went to the granary and feasted on those delicious eggs.

In the end, there was only one egg left.

Hare thought he'd better bring his visit to an end. So that evening he said to Crocodile, "I think I'll go home tomorrow. I've loved being here, but there are a number of things I must do at home. I'm sure you understand." And Crocodile said yes, of course, and they'd loved having him.

In the morning they were about to leave, for Crocodile had to take Hare across the water on his back, when Crocodile said, "I must just count the eggs before we go. I always count them at this time of year."

"Oh, eggs!" said Hare. "You have eggs, have you? I never knew you had eggs! Eggs, eh? Where do you keep them?" He felt dreadfully nervous.

"They're kept in the granary," said Crocodile. "Haven't you noticed them?"

"Noticed them!" said Hare. "Goodness me, no! I had no idea! How many are there?"

"There are exactly seventy," said Crocodile.

"I'd like to see them for myself," said Hare.

"So you shall," said Crocodile. "In fact, if you like, you can count them for me."

"Nothing would please me more," said Hare. (And he meant it.) He climbed into the granary and then into the corner where the eggs were kept. "Oh," he cried. "What wonderful eggs! Oh what fine big, yellow eggs! I say, I shall enjoy counting these!"

And he took the one remaining egg and lifted it up so Crocodile could see it. And then Hare started counting. "One," he said, and lowered the egg to the bottom of the bin. Then he lifted the egg again, so Crocodile could see it, and said, "Two." He lowered it to the bottom of the bin, and lifted it again. "Three." And so he went on. ". . . Fifteen, sixteen . . ." he said. Sometimes he would stay down for a time, as if he was taking an egg from the far side of the bin. ". . . Thirty-one, thirty-two . . ." he said. And at last he came to: ". . . Sixty-nine, *seventy!*"

"Exactly seventy," he called.

"Yes, I told you we had exactly seventy eggs," said Crocodile. "Well, that's done, then. They're all safe." And after they'd said goodbye to Hare's sister, they set off for the lakeside. When they came to the water, Hare climbed on Crocodile's back, and Crocodile began swimming to the mainland, where Hare lived.

But not long after they'd gone, Crocodile's wife went into the granary to check for herself that the eggs were all there. She climbed into the bin. Horror! Only one egg left! She rushed at once to the edge of the lake. Half-way across to the mainland she could see a splashing, and she knew that was Crocodile, swimming with Hare on his back. At the top of her voice she cried, "Crocodile, Crocodile, Hare has eaten nearly all our eggs! He has eaten them all but one! Throw him in the lake! Drown him, drown him!"

"Is that my wife calling?" said Crocodile. "It's so windy, I can't make out what she's saying."

"I can hear her very well," said Hare.

"What is she saying, then?"

"She's saying you could swim even faster if you wanted, because there's a strong wind behind us," said Hare.

"Oh, good," said Crocodile. "Then I *will* swim faster, and you will get home sooner, my friend."

And he did that, and Hare did get home sooner. They said goodbye, and Crocodile set off to swim home again.

But I have to tell you that Hare didn't think it wise to stay in his home a day longer. For some reason, he went to live far away, and when people asked him if his sister wasn't married to Crocodile, he'd pretend he was deaf, and hadn't heard what they said.

THE LITTLE DRUMMER

The Brothers Grimm

One evening a little drummer was going home, and he came to a lake. And there on the shore of the lake he found a piece of fine white linen. He put it in his pocket, and then made for home, still drumming.

When he was in bed, about to fall asleep, he heard a young woman's voice calling in the darkness, "Little drummer! Don't go to sleep yet! Listen to me!"

"I *am* listening," cried the little drummer. "Who are you?"

"Please, *please*," said the voice. "*Please* give me back my dress! Give me back the dress you found by the lake!"

"Why," said the drummer, "was that your dress? I'm sorry. I wouldn't have taken it if I'd known. But please tell me who you are."

"I am a king's daughter," said the voice. "I fell into the power of an old witch, and she keeps me shut up on the top of a great mountain – a glass mountain. Every night I have to bathe in the lake. But I can't go back without my dress. Please give it to me."

"Of course," said the little drummer. The linen was by his bed. "But where are you?"

"I'm here in the darkness," said the princess's voice. "That's it! I have it! Thank you, little drummer. And now I must go."

"Wait," cried the little drummer. "Is there nothing I can do to help you?"

"You can do nothing," said the voice, sadly. "To help me you would have to climb to the top of the glass mountain. But you wouldn't even be able to find it. And if you did, you would never reach the top."

"Princess," cried the little drummer, "I am not afraid of anything. Tell me how to get to the mountain."

The voice was fading. "The mountain is at the end of the road through the forest," it said, "where the giants live. That's all I can tell you. I dare not stay longer. Goodbye, little drummer. Goodbye!" And the voice had gone.

The little drummer hardly slept at all that night. He kept thinking of the poor princess, and wondering how he might save her from the old witch. As soon as it was light he leapt out of bed and buckled on his drum. Then, without a word to anyone, he crept out of the house and made straight for the forest. No one had been there for a long time, for fear of the giants who had made their home in it. But in among the trees the little drummer went. He could hear birds, and the sound of leaves as the morning breeze shook the trees. He saw many small animals. But of the giants there was no sight and no sound.

But he had to find a giant if he was to get to the glass mountain. What could he do?

And then he thought of his drum. Yes, he'd use his drum to wake them up!

At the sound of the drumming the birds flew out of the trees. But for a long time nothing else happened at all. The leaves rustled in the breeze. Nothing was to be seen. And then . . . There was a great stirring. There was a creaking and cracking of branches. And the earth shook. Then out

from among the trees, stretching and yawning, came a giant, taller than the tallest tree in the forest.

"You miserable midget!" he roared. "You noisy dwarf! How dare you beat on that drum! You woke me up before I was ready for it!" And he yawned and scowled.

"I'm sorry, giant," said the little drummer, "but I have to play my drum. How else can I let the others know the way?"

"The others?" roared the giant. "What others?"

"Well," said the little drummer, "all the thousands upon thousands who are following me."

"Thousands upon thousands?" growled the giant. "Thousands upon thousands like you? What are thousands upon thousands of midgets doing in my forest?"

"Well," said the little drummer, "if you really want to know, we've come to find you and your friends and put an end to you all. You make the forest unsafe for us, you see. I'm afraid we have to get rid of you."

The giant laughed, and the trees shook. "It would take more than thousands upon thousands of midgets to get rid of me and my friends," he roared. "Why, we'd pick up each midget between our fingers and our thumbs and crush him like a grasshopper."

It was the little drummer's turn to laugh. "Have you ever tried to pick up a grasshopper, giant?" he asked. "As soon as you bent down to pick one of us up . . . with one hop he'd have gone. And you'd never find him again in the trees and bushes. And then what would happen when you grew tired and had to sleep? Then we'd all come creeping out and . . . Well, I don't have to tell you what would happen. I'm sorry, giant. But it has to be done."

And the little drummer was so bold that the giant was frightened. "Oh, now, look here, little drummer," he said, in the quietest voice he could manage. "I and my friends never meant any harm. It's been a misunderstanding. If you'll run back and tell the other midgets to go away, we'll leave you alone in future. I give you my promise."

"Well, I don't know," said the little drummer.

"And look," said the giant, "if there's anything I can do for *you* now, just tell me. I'll be glad to do it."

"There is something you could do, giant," said the little drummer. "I want to get to the glass mountain. If you promise to carry me there on your back, I'll give my friends a signal on my drum and they will all go home."

"To the glass mountain?" said the giant. "Of course! Easy! You give that signal and we'll be off!"

So the little drummer beat on his drum, and then he climbed onto the giant's back, up on his shoulders and onto the rim of his hat, and they set off.

The drummer walked to and fro and round and round on the rim of the giant's hat, peering in all directions. At last, over the trees, he saw the tip of a great mountain. It shone in the sun like a huge block of ice. In two more strides they were at the foot of the mountain, and the giant's hand came up and took the drummer from the rim of his hat and set him on the ground.

The little drummer called out at once that he wanted to be taken to the very top of the mountain. But the giant shook his head. To climb up there was more than even he could do. He turned back into the forest and disappeared.

The little drummer could see at once that it was useless to think of climbing the mountain. It wasn't just that it was so high. Its sides were as smooth as ice. He sat on the ground, his chin in his hands, and wondered what to do.

And then he heard a noise. He looked round and saw that not far away two men were fighting, fiercely. He hurried towards them and saw that on the ground beside

them was a saddle. And as they struggled and beat each other they shouted.

"It's my turn," shouted one. "You know it's my turn on the saddle! Just give in and let me have it!"

"That's not true," shouted the other. "It's mine!"

"Hey, stop!" cried the little drummer. "What are you doing? What's the sense of fighting over a saddle when you haven't got a horse to put it on?"

"A horse?" said the first man, not letting go of the other's arms. "You don't need a horse for this saddle. If you want to go somewhere – anywhere – you have only to sit on the saddle and wish yourself where you want to go. And hey presto, there you are!"

"Whose saddle is it?" asked the little drummer.

"It belongs to both of us," said the man. "And it's my turn to sit on it!"

"You're a liar!" cried the other, twisting and kicking.

"Now look here," said the little drummer. "Don't start fighting again. I know how to settle this. Do you see this stick? I'll run over there" – he pointed to a spot a few yards away – "and I'll push the stick in the ground. See? Then both of you run to the stick. And the one who gets there first has the next ride on the saddle. What do you say?"

"Aye, that's fair, drummer," said one of the men.

"Yes, drummer, that's fair," said the other.

So the little drummer ran to the spot he'd pointed to, and stuck the stick in the ground. Then he returned to where the men were standing, by the saddle. "Are you ready, then?" he called. "Ready – steady – *go!*"

And off they ran. But they hadn't gone more than a couple of steps before the drummer had jumped on the saddle and wished he was at the top of the mountain.

And at once, there he was.

It was flat up there. It was cold and flat and strange. Not far away from where he stood was an old house built of black stone. There was a great fishpond in front of it. Behind the house was a forest, deep and dark. There was no one to be seen. All that could be heard was the wail of the wind in the trees. The little drummer shivered.

Then he plucked up courage and made his way to the house. The door was black, like the rest of the house. The little drummer knocked, and waited.

There was a shuffling inside the house, and then, very slowly, the door opened. Standing there was an old woman. Her face was brown and wrinkled like the shell of a walnut. Her eyes were wicked and red.

"And what do you want, little drummer?" she asked. Her voice was as sharp as a needle.

"If you please," said the little drummer, "I'd be glad of something to eat. And a bed for the night."

"Hmm. Well, yes," said the witch, and now her voice was as sharp as a knife. "You shall have food and a bed. But only if you'll do three things for me in return."

"Of course I will," said the little drummer. "What are the three things?"

"Come in, little drummer," said the witch. She held the black door open, and the drummer saw that the inside of the house was black, too. "I can see you are hungry and tired. Eat and sleep. In the morning, I'll tell you what the first of the three things is."

So the little drummer went into the blackness inside the black stone house. The old woman gave him a meal and then he went to his bed, in a small dark room with a tiny window that looked out on the black edge of the forest.

In the morning the old woman gave him his breakfast. Then she took a thimble from her finger and held it out.

"Take this, little drummer," she said. "And here is the first thing I want you to do. I want you to empty my fishpond with this thimble. It must be done before nightfall."

"Is that . . . all?" asked the little drummer.

The old woman cackled. "No," she said, and now her voice was as sharp as a sword. "It's not quite all. I want the fish you find in the pond, all of them, laid out on the bank, very carefully side by side."

"And is that . . . all?" asked the little drummer.

Again the old woman cackled. "No, that's not all, either. I want all the fish of the same kind laid together. You understand?"

"I understand," said the little drummer. "But . . ."

"One last thing," said the witch. "Of all the fish of each kind, I want all the fish of the same size laid together. And I'll be back at nightfall to see that you've done it."

And she seemed to vanish, cackling, into the forest.

The little drummer didn't see how he could begin. Empty a whole fishpond with one little thimble? But there was nothing to do but try. All morning he baled away at the dark water, but when midday came, the pond seemed as full as ever. As for the fish, he could see them under the dark surface, thousands of them, swimming to and fro. He had not landed one of them.

He sat down by the edge of the pond. If he'd not been so brave, he'd have wept. And at that moment a girl came out of the house, carrying food in a basket. She was very beautiful.

"Here, little drummer," she said. "This food is for you. But why do you sit there so sadly?"

"I'm sad," said the little drummer, "because I can't finish the first task the old woman gave me to do. I can't even begin it! And there are still two more tasks to be done! Worse than that! I came to find a king's daughter who is kept a prisoner here, and I haven't done that, either."

"Listen, little drummer," said the girl. "I can help you. You're very tired after all the work you've done. Look, I'll sit beside you. Lay your head in my lap, and go to sleep. When you wake up, I promise you, the work will be done."

The little drummer was tired, no doubt of that. He did as the girl had told him, and as soon as his eyes were shut, she turned a ring on her finger. At once strange things began to happen. The water in the lake turned into mist and then into a great cloud. The cloud rose high in the air and drifted away. As for the fish, they leapt from the pond and laid themselves down on the shore in heaps, according to their kind and their size.

Then the little drummer woke up.

"Why," he cried. "The pond is empty. And the fish are laid in heaps as the old woman ordered. How can I thank you for helping me?"

"Never mind about that," said the girl. "The task is

129

done. But look, little drummer. There's one fish over there lying by itself. When the old woman comes tonight, she'll say, 'Why is this fish lying on its own?' And when she says that, throw it in her face and say, 'This one is for you, old witch.' Do as I tell you, and all will be well."

And that evening when the witch came the little drummer did as the girl had told him. He threw the fish in the witch's face, but she said nothing, and only gave him an angry glare.

The next morning she told him his second task.

"The work I gave you yesterday was too easy, little drummer," she said. Her voice was now sharper than knives, sharper than swords. "It was far too easy. Today I want you to cut down all the trees in the forest."

"Is that all?" asked the little drummer.

The old woman cackled horribly. "No, that's not quite all," she said. "I want you to split the wood into logs, and it must all be done by tonight. Here is an axe, and here is a mallet, and here are two wedges. Take them. Remember, I shall be here when night falls to see that you've done it."

And again she seemed to vanish into the blackness of the forest.

The little drummer didn't see how he could begin such a task. It was worse than emptying the pond. How could one man cut down a whole forest? How could he split all that wood into logs? But there was nothing to do but try. So he set to work. But he soon found that the axe the witch had given him was made of soft metal, and the mallet and the wedges were of tin. So the edge of the axe was soon blunt, and the mallet and the wedges twisted out of shape.

When midday came he sat down on the ground. It was hard not to weep. And again the beautiful girl came out of the house with food in a basket.

130

"Don't be sad, little drummer," she cried. "Lay your head on my lap again, and sleep, and when you wake the work will be done."

The little drummer did as she told him. As soon as his eyes were shut, she turned the ring on her finger, and at once strange things began to happen. Every tree in the forest fell down, and the wood split itself into logs. Then the little drummer woke up.

"Why!" he cried. "The whole forest is cut down. And the wood is split into logs! How can I thank you for helping me?"

"Never mind about that," said the girl. "The task is done. But look, little drummer. There is one branch over there lying by itself, not cut up. When the old woman comes tonight, she'll say, 'Why is this branch lying by itself, and why is it not cut up?' When she says that, give her a blow with the branch and say, 'That's for you, old witch.' Do as I tell you, and all will be well."

And that evening when the witch came the little drummer did as the girl had told him. And when he gave the witch a blow with the branch, she said nothing. She only gave him a glare from her wicked red eyes.

The next morning the witch told the little drummer what his third task was to be.

"The work I gave you yesterday," she said, "was too easy. Today I want you to put all the logs in one great heap."

"Is that all?" asked the little drummer.

"No. That's not quite all," said the witch. "I want you to set fire to the heap and burn it to ashes. At night I shall come to see that it's done."

And she vanished cackling into the forest.

The little drummer didn't see how he could begin such a task. It was worse than emptying the pond or cutting down the forest. How could one man heap up all those logs and burn them to ashes? But there was nothing to do but try. All the morning he carried logs and heaped them up. But when midday came you could hardly see the work he'd done. It made so small a pile. He sat down on the ground, and tried not to cry.

And again the beautiful girl came with food for him, and again she told him to lay his head on her lap and sleep. Then she turned the ring on her finger, and at once strange things began to happen. All the logs leapt into one great pile, and the pile began to burn fiercely.

And the little drummer woke up.

"Why!" he cried. "All the logs are in one great pile, and the pile is burning fiercely. How can I thank you for helping me?"

"Never mind about that," said the girl. "The task is done. Now listen, little drummer. When the witch comes tonight, she will give you an order. Do whatever she says, without the smallest fear. You will be safe, whatever happens. And when you have done it, then seize her and throw her into the flames."

When night came, the witch appeared. "So you have done as I asked you," she cried. "Ah, what a good fire this is! It warms the bones of a poor old woman like me. But there is one log that's not burning – there, right in the middle. Go in there, little drummer, and bring it out to me. Once you've done that, you will be free to go wherever you wish. Go along! Into the fire and bring out the log!"

The little drummer remembered what the girl had told him. So, though the heat was great and the flames were high, he leapt into the fire with no fear at all. It roared round him, but without hurting him. He seized the log, carried it out of the fire and laid it on the ground.

And as he did so, suddenly the beautiful girl was standing before him. Now she was wearing robes of silk and gold. He knew at once that she was the king's daughter.

But the old witch hopped up and down cackling.

"You think you've got her safe, little drummer," she screeched. "But you haven't! I shall take her away!"

"Oh no, you won't, old witch!" cried the little drummer. "I shall get you first!"

And at once he seized the old woman with both hands. He raised her above his head and threw her into the fire.

Then the princess led the little drummer into the house, and there he saw great chests crammed with treasure. They left the gold and silver, for it was too heavy to carry. They took only the precious stones. And then the little drummer said, "Let's get on my saddle, and in the twinkling of an eye we shall be at the bottom of the mountain."

But the princess smiled and said, "Why bother with your saddle? I have only to twist my ring – like this – and . . ."

And there they were – in the palace of the king, her father. Where, very soon, you won't be surprised to hear, the princess and the little drummer were married.

And all the drummers in the kingdom played at their wedding feast.

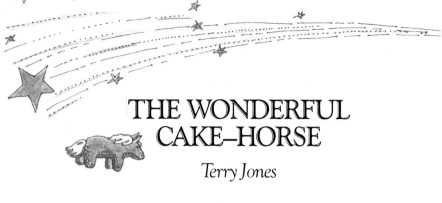

THE WONDERFUL CAKE–HORSE

Terry Jones

A man once made a cake shaped like a horse. That night a shooting star flew over the house and a spark happened to fall on the cake-horse. Well, the cake-horse lay there for a few moments. Then it gave a snort. Then it whinnied, scrambled to its legs, and shook its mane of white icing, and stood there in the moonlight, gazing round at the world.

The man, who was asleep in bed, heard the noise and looked out of the window, and saw his cake-horse running around the garden, bucking and snorting, just as if it had been a real wild horse.

"Cake-horse!" cried the man. "What are you doing?"

"Aren't I a fine horse!" cried the cake-horse. "You can ride me if you like."

But the man said, "You've got no horseshoes and you've got no saddle, and you're only made of cake!"

The cake-horse snorted and bucked and kicked the air, and galloped across the garden, and leapt clean over the gate, and disappeared into the night.

The next morning, the cake-horse went to the nearby town, and said to the blacksmith, "Blacksmith, make me some horseshoes, for my feet are only made of cake."

But the blacksmith said, "How will you pay me?"

And the cake-horse answered, "If you make me some horseshoes, I'll be your friend."

But the blacksmith shook his head: "I don't need friends like that!" he said.

So the cake-horse galloped to the saddler, and said, "Saddler! Make me a saddle of the best leather – one that will go with my icing-sugar mane!"

But the saddler said, "If I make you a saddle, how will you pay me?"

"I'll be your friend," said the cake-horse.

"I don't need friends like that!" said the saddler, and shook his head.

The cake-horse snorted and bucked and kicked its legs in the air and said, "Why doesn't anyone want to be my friend? I'll go and join the wild horses!" And he galloped off to the moors where the wild horses roamed.

But when he saw the other wild horses, they were all so big and wild that he was afraid they would trample him to crumbs without even noticing he was there.

Just then he came upon a mouse who was groaning to himself under a stone.

"What's the matter with you?" asked the cake-horse.

"Oh," said the mouse, "I ran away from my home in the town, and came up here where there is nothing to eat, and now I'm dying of hunger and too weak to get back."

The cake-horse felt very sorry for the mouse, so it said, "Here you are! You can nibble a bit of me, if you like, for I'm made of cake."

"That's most kind of you," said the mouse, and he ate a little of the cake-horse's tail, and a little of his icing-sugar mane. "Now I feel much better."

Then the cake-horse said, "If only I had a saddle and some horseshoes, I could carry you back to the town."

"*I'll* make you them," said the mouse, and he made four little horseshoes out of acorn-cups, and a saddle out of beetle-shells, and he got up on the cake-horse's back and rode him back to town.

And there they remained the best of friends for the rest of their lives.

TIM RABBIT

Alison Uttley

The wind howled and the rain poured down in torrents. A young rabbit hurried along with his eyes half shut and his head bent as he forced his way against the gale. He tore his trousers on a bramble and left a piece of his coat on a gorse-bush. He bumped his nose and scratched his chin, but he didn't stop to rub himself. He hurried and scurried towards the snug little house on the common where his mother was making bread.

At last he saw the open door, he smelled the warm smell of baking, and in he rushed without wiping his feet on the little brown doormat.

"What's the matter, Tim?" asked Mrs Rabbit, as she shut the oven door. "Whatever has happened?" She looked anxiously at Tim who lay panting on the floor.

"Something came after me," cried Tim, breathlessly.

"Something came after you?" echoed Mrs Rabbit. "What was it like, my son?"

"It was very big and noisy," replied Tim, with a shiver. "It ran all round me, and tried to pull the coat off my back, and it snatched at my trousers." He gave a sob, and his mother stroked his head.

"What did it say?" she asked. "Did it speak or growl?"

"It called, 'Whoo-oo-oo. Whoo-oo-oo. Whoo-oo-oo,'" whimpered the little rabbit.

"That was only the wind, my son," said Mrs Rabbit, with a laugh. "Never fear the wind, for he is a friend." She gave the little rabbit a crust of new bread, and he was comforted.

The next day, when Tim Rabbit was nibbling a morsel of sweet grass under the hedge, the sky darkened, and a hailstorm swept across the sky, with stinging hailstones. They bounced on the small rabbit and frightened him out of his wits. Off he ran, helter-skelter, with his white tail bobbing, and his eyes wide with fear. He lost his pocket handkerchief and left his scarf in a thicket, but he hadn't time to pick them up, he was in such a hurry.

He raced and he tore towards the snug little house on the common, where his mother was tossing pancakes and catching them in her tiny stone frying-pan.

At last he reached the door, and in he raced without stopping to smooth his rough untidy hair.

"What's the matter, Tim?" asked Mrs Rabbit, as she put down her frying-pan. "Whatever is the matter?"

"Something came after me," exclaimed Tim, hiding behind her skirts.

"Something came after you?" cried Mrs Rabbit. "What was it like?"

"It was big and dark," said Tim. "It threw hard stones at me, and hit my nose and back and ears. It must have a hundred paws, to throw so many stones, and every time it hit me and hurt me."

"What did it say?" asked Mrs Rabbit, lifting her son from the floor, and straightening his ruffled hair.

"It shouted, 'Whissh-ssh-ssh! Whissh-ssh-ssh!'" sobbed the little rabbit.

"That was only a hail-storm, Tim," explained Mrs Rabbit. "Never heed a hail-storm, for it clears the air, and makes all fresh for us rabbits." She gave the little rabbit a curly yellow pancake with some sugar on the top, and he forgot his troubles.

The next day when Tim was tasting an early primrose, the first he had seen in his short life, he had another fright. A thunder-storm broke out of the sky, with lightning which flashed around him, and peals of roaring thunder which echoed from the hills.

Tim scampered home as fast as his legs could carry him, to the warm little house on the common, where his mother was toasting currant teacakes in front of the wood fire.

At last he came to the door, and the smell of the teacakes made his whiskers twitch. He rushed inside, without stopping to shake the wet from his coat.

"What's the matter, Tim?" cried Mrs Rabbit, as he stumbled into a chair. She dropped her toasting-fork and leaned over him. "What's the matter, my son?"

"Something came after me," whispered Tim, shuddering.

"Something came after you?" echoed his mother. "What was it like?"

"It was very big and high," cried Tim. "It stuck bright swords at me, and flashed lights in my eyes."

"What did it say?" asked Mrs Rabbit softly.

"It roared 'Roo-oo-oo-oo-oo!'" wept the little rabbit.

"That was only a thunder-storm, my son," replied Mrs Rabbit, soothingly. "Never mind the thunder and lightning. They never harmed a rabbit yet." She gave him a large teacake, and he sat by the fire munching it, with his troubles forgotten.

But there came a day when Tim Rabbit sat dozing in a clump of ferns, half asleep, and comfortable. A gust of wind brought a queer scent to his nostrils and he awoke suddenly. He stared round and saw a strange animal bounding towards him with joyous leaps. It wasn't a lamb, nor a foal, nor a calf, nor even a pigling. It looked so playful and danced along so merrily on its four hairy legs that Tim wanted to play Catch, and Hide-and-seek.

What a jolly creature it was! How curly was its hair and its long waving tail! It hadn't seen Tim, for the ferns covered him, but he was prepared to run out and meet it. He would have invited it home, if a storm hadn't suddenly swept down from a dark cloud which hung in the sky.

"Beware! Beware!" howled the wind, and it blew Tim's fur the wrong way, until he was uncomfortable and cold.

"Shoo! Shoo!" sighed the trees, waving their branches and crackling their twigs at him, like tiny wooden fingers.

"Run! Run!" cried the bushes, snapping and rustling their spiky boughs, with the prickly thorns.

"Be off! Be off!" roared the thunder, banging its drum inside the black cloud.

The lightning flashed and showed him the sharp teeth of the merry dancing animal. The hailstones rattled down and hit foolish Tim's nose, so that he turned and ran, leaving the creature to play by itself in the wet field.

He scuttled towards the safe little house on the common, where his mother was making crab-apple tart. He ran in at the door, and flopped down on the oak bench.

"What's the matter, Tim?" asked his mother, dropping her rolling-pin and scattering the bowl of crab-apples. "Whatever is the matter, my son?"

"Mother, I saw an animal. It was not a lamb, nor a foal, nor a calf, nor a pigling, but a lovely jumping animal. I was going to play with it, but the wind blew me, and the hailstones hit me, and the thunder scolded me, and they all drove me home."

"What was it like, my son?" asked Mrs Rabbit, as she wiped the floor, and picked up her crab-apples.

"It was white, with kind eyes, and long ears and shining teeth, Mother, and its paws danced and pattered."

"What did it say, Tim?" cried Mrs Rabbit, faintly.

"It said, 'Bow-wow! Bow-wow!'"

"That was a dog, Tim," whispered Mrs Rabbit, in a frightened tone. "Beware of a dog! He would have killed you with his sharp teeth and pattering paws."

So the little rabbit sat on his stool in the chimney corner, warming his toes by the fire, whilst he learned his first lesson:

> "Crouch among the heather,
> Never mind the weather,
> Forget it altogether.
> Run from a dog, a man, and a gun,
> Or your happy young life will soon be undone."

TOBY, THE BEANS
AND THE HEDGEHOG

Nancy Blishen

Have you ever thought what it must have been like to be a child sixty years ago? So much would have been different! Well, here's a story, and it's true, about a little girl called Hannah, who was six at the time.

She lived with her father and mother near London, and her best friend was her dog Toby. Toby's father had been an Alsatian, and his mother a Corgi. So Toby was a rather funny shape. He had a long body, rather like a sausage, very short legs, a head like an Alsatian's with long pointed ears, and a great feathery tail. When Hannah took him for a walk in long grass, all you could see of Toby was his ears and the tip of that feathery tail.

Hannah's Granny and Grandpa lived in the country and sometimes she went to stay there, always taking Toby with her. Hannah loved Granny's house. It smelt of apples; and instead of electric light, there were oil lamps. But what she liked best of all was going to bed. You may think this strange. Most boys and girls of six I know will try anything to put off going to bed. But there was something special about going to bed in Granny's house. If it was winter Granny would say, "Time to get down the warming pan!" Then Hannah would carefully lift down, from its hook by

the fire, something that was made of copper, had a long wooden handle, and looked like a very flat saucepan. Granny would go to the fire and, with the tongs, take out several hot coals. She'd put these in the pan, close the lid and, with a flickering candle in her hand, take Hannah upstairs. Then she'd rub the warming pan over the big, fluffy bed, and Hannah would jump into that warm nest. She'd sink down into the feathers until nothing could be seen of her but the tip of her nose.

But the story I want to tell you is about something that happened in summer time. Round Granny's house, wrapped all the way round it, was a beautiful big garden. Grandpa was enormously proud of his flowers and vegetables. He was especially proud of his runner beans. They climbed up poles – rows and rows and rows of them, all very straight and neat.

One day Hannah was filling her pocket with nuts from a tree at the end of the garden when she noticed that some of the bean plants were behaving oddly. They were wobbling and jumping about. Some were even leaning sideways! She hurried to the spot and – oh, dear! There was Toby, feathery tail and all, digging an enormous hole right in the middle of Grandpa's rows of beans. And right in the middle of that enormous hole was a little hedgehog, curled up tight, a prickly ball.

Now, Hannah knew that Granny and Grandpa were asleep in their armchairs. They were having what Granny called forty winks, though it sometimes went on so long that Hannah thought they might have been fifty or sixty winks, or even seventy. Anyway, there was time, surely, before they woke, to do something about Toby and the beans and the hedgehog. So she rushed off and got her little garden spade and gently lifted the hedgehog out of the hole. He scuttled off into the bushes, looking very put out, while Hannah held on to Toby's collar so he could not follow.

"Oh, Toby, how could you?" cried Hannah. And Toby dropped his ears and his tail and looked very sorry for himself. He'd been having a good time. What was wrong with that?

Hannah filled in the hole as best she could and straightened up the beans; and then she took Toby back to the house just as the kettle on the fire began to boil, ready for tea. Grandpa said:

"I think I'll go and water my beans before it gets dark. I'll be back in no time for a cup of tea and a slice of that cherry cake I saw you taking out of the oven this morning."

Well, poor Hannah! She loved Grandpa very much. But sometimes his eyes were fierce under his bushy white eyebrows. She wondered if he'd guess it was Toby who had disturbed his beans. She heard his footsteps going through the kitchen, and the back door opening and shutting. She waited, trembling. And after what seemed ages she heard the back door open again, and shut, and Grandpa's voice. "That wretched cat from next door! He's been scratching about among my beans!" And she heard Granny say, "Oh dear! Oh dear!"

And Hannah breathed an enormous sigh of relief and took a very large bite of cherry cake. As for Toby, he looked out from under the table where he'd been hiding and closed one eye. It looked for all the world as though he were winking.

And if you're wondering how I know about this – well, I was Hannah!

THE MUSICIANS OF BREMEN

The Brothers Grimm

There was once a donkey. He wasn't young, for he'd spent much of his life working for a farmer. He'd plodded and carried, as donkeys do. He'd taken sacks of corn to the mill, and sacks of flour back to the farm. And he'd never complained! But the day came when his old bones would carry no more sacks. He hoped he would be able to spend his last years quietly and comfortably in some corner of the farm. But the farmer was not a good man.

"Ah," he said. "So you can't work any more, eh? More than one sack and you're on your knees! Well, an old donkey is an idle donkey, and an idle donkey is no good to me. So . . . off you go! You can find your own way in the world now!"

And off the poor donkey trotted, out through the farmyard gate and into the road. There he stopped, and asked himself what he should do now.

"What *can* I do?" he thought. "I've never learned to do anything but carry sacks of corn and sacks of flour for that miserable, ungrateful farmer. All I'm good for now is eating and drinking and thinking about the good days when I was young." And he was so unhappy that he brayed, loudly.

And then an idea struck him.

"Wait a minute!" he thought. "Let me try that again!"

And again he brayed, but this time more quietly. "Hmm!" he thought. "That's music! I've never thought of it before! It's rather a nice sound!" And he brayed again, this time not loud, but not quiet, either. "I'm a musician!" he cried. "Yes, that's a very fine sound!" And he began to make his way slowly down the road, trying out his voice.

"Well," he cried. "That's a problem solved! Now I know what to do. I'll become a musician. I'll go to the nearest city – that's Bremen – I went there once or twice with my master. Yes, yes, yes, that's what I'll do!"

And off he trotted, practising his music as he went. He'd gone about a mile when he saw a dog lying by the roadside. The dog had the saddest look about him.

"Ah, hallo, dog," said the donkey. "What are you looking so miserable about?" And the dog howled.

"Oh, I'm old," he cried. "I'm old and I can't hunt any more. I can't smell things properly, you see. And I can't run too well. So my master's driven me away. After all the years I've hunted for him – *and* looked after his house at night! How I'm going to keep alive I don't know. I never could do anything but hunt – and look after houses – and bury bones." And he howled again.

"Hmm, cheer up," said the donkey. "I think I know the answer to your problem. Do that again."

"Do what?" said the dog.

"Make that noise you made," said the donkey.

"What, this?" said the dog, and he howled.

"Fine!" said the donkey. "A most interesting sound! You're a musician too, you know!"

"A musician?" said the dog, and he barked with surprise.

"Ah, that's even better," said the donkey. "I can see you've got more than one piece of music in you. You know, you're a very *clever* musician! Look, this is my plan! I'm going to Bremen to make my living as a singer. You come

along with me and – why, we could sing duets. We'll be the talk of the town!"

The dog growled. "Oh, all right," he said. "It sounds better than just lying here." And off they went together, practising their music as they went.

They'd gone another mile or so when they came across a very unhappy-looking cat. The cat was sitting by the road, too sad, it seemed, even to clean itself. It was rather dusty, and there was a dead leaf hanging from one whisker.

"Oh hallo, cat," said the donkey. "What are you looking so dismal about?"

The cat miaowed, sadly. "Oh, I'm old," she said. "I'm old and there's no edge to my teeth any more. And even if there were, my sight's that bad that I can't tell a mouse from a . . . mowing-machine. Haven't caught one for a whole year. Haven't even seen one for six months! So my mistress has driven me away. After all the mice I caught for her when I was young! And the games I played with her children, and the way I kept her lap warm in the winter evenings! How I'm going to earn my living, I don't know. I can't do anything but drink milk and sit snoring by the fire." And she miaowed again, most miserably.

"Hmm, cheer up," said the donkey. "I think I know the answer to your problem. Do that again."

"Do what?" asked the cat.

"Make that noise you made."

"What, this?" asked the cat. And she miaowed. It was a sound that would have broken your heart.

"Splendid!" cried the donkey. "That will bring tears to the eyes of the people of Bremen! A lovely sound, isn't it?"

And the cat miaowed again, and listened to the sound she made. "Well, yes," she said. "I hadn't thought about it. It *is* rather lovely, I suppose."

"No supposing about it," said the donkey. "I could listen to it all day. Very charming! Cat, you're a musician too!"

"A musician?" cried the cat. And this time she purred, with pleasure.

"Oh, listen to *that*!" cried the donkey. "What superb singing! How do you manage so many different notes? Isn't it superb, dog?"

"Most superb, donkey," said the dog.

And the donkey explained their plan – to go to Bremen and make their living as musicians. "Why," he said, "if you come along with us, cat, we could sing trios!"

The cat miaowed and said, "Oh, very well. It will be better than just lying around trying to smell mice that aren't there."

So off they went together, practising their music.

They'd gone another mile or so when they saw on a gatepost a cockerel with his feathers drooping miserably. His fine red comb was flopping about his head in the unhappiest way.

"Ah, hallo, cockerel," said the donkey. "What are you looking so dreary about?"

The cockerel crowed – a very cracked sort of crow.

"Oh, I'm old," he said. "My happy days in the farmyard are over. My mistress is going to wring my neck and have me for dinner tomorrow. After all the times I've crowed in the morning to tell her it's time to wake up! Better than a clock I've been to her, and all she can think of is to wring my neck! Would you be happy if all you had to look forward to was being eaten? I don't know what I shall do. All I can do is crow." And he crowed again.

"Hmm, cheer up," said the donkey. "I think I know the answer to your problem. Do that again."

"Do what?" said the cockerel.

151

"Make that noise you made."

"What, this?" And the cockerel crowed.

"Magnificent," cried the donkey. "Isn't it a wonderful sound?"

"Most wonderful!" cried the dog and the cat together.

"You have great talent, my friend," said the donkey. "You see, you're a musician, too."

"A musician?" cried the cockerel. And he was so astonished that he crowed again.

"Oh, that *wonderful* sound!" cried the donkey. And he explained their plan – to make their way to Bremen and earn their living as musicians. "Why," he said. "If you come too, cockerel, we could sing quartets!"

The cockerel crowed, thought, and then crowed again.

"Oh, all right," he said. "It's better than being roasted and eaten, anyway."

So off they went together, the donkey, the dog, the cat and the cockerel, practising their music as they went.

But it was a long road to Bremen, and there was still far to go when night began to fall. The road ran into a forest, and it was black under the trees, and a cold wind blew. They decided they must rest for the night. So the donkey lay under a tall tree, the dog lay beside him, the cat climbed up among the branches, saying it was safer there, and the cockerel flew to the very top of the tree, saying he wouldn't feel safe any lower down.

In fact, the cockerel was so nervous that before he settled he looked this way, and that way, and in front of him, and behind him, to make sure all was well. To the north there was nothing but blackness to be seen, and the same to the east and west. But when he looked to the south, there, not far away, was a small, warm light.

"I see a light!" he called. "A friendly-looking light!"

"That means a house," cried the donkey. "Well, if it's not far as a donkey walks . . ."

". . . or a dog . . ." said the dog.

". . . or a cat . . ." said the cat.

"Then we'll go," said the donkey. "We could do with something to eat."

"And somewhere comfortable to sleep," said the dog.

"And a nice warm fire," said the cat.

So they gave up the idea of sleeping in the forest and set off towards the light the cockerel had seen. Soon they came to a clearing, and in it was a small cottage, with a light shining out of its window. The animals crept out of the trees, and into the garden of the cottage. The donkey, being the tallest, gently laid his front hooves on the windowsill and peeped inside.

"What can you see?" asked the cockerel.

"Hmm. Food," said the donkey, "heaps of food!"

"Hurrah," said the cat.

"And drink! Plenty to drink!"

"Fine," said the dog.

"All set on a table, ready to eat."

"Good, good!" cried the cockerel.

"And more in the oven, by the looks of it!"

"I can't wait," cried the cat.

"And a nice warm fire!"

"Wonderful!" said the dog.

"And round the table, eating and drinking . . ."

"A kind old lady, who likes giving milk to cats?" said the cat, eagerly.

"And a kind old man, who loves giving bones to dogs?" said the dog, his mouth watering.

"They love animals – especially cockerels," said the cockerel.

153

"And they love music, too," said the cat.

"Let's go in," said the dog.

"No, no, you're all quite wrong!" said the donkey. "It's a band of robbers having their dinner!"

"Oh, *robbers*!" said the others.

"I don't fancy that," said the dog.

"Not my idea of nice people at all," said the cat.

"Well, that's that. Back to the forest," said the cockerel.

"I could almost taste that bone," said the dog.

"I could feel the milk going down, rich and creamy," said the cat.

"What I was thinking of," said the cockerel, "was corn. Rather a lot of corn . . ."

"Wait a minute!" said the donkey. He got down from the windowsill. "Wait a minute! I've got a plan. Now, listen!"

And, there in the cottage garden, they put their heads together, and the donkey told them his plan. It was all they could do not to bark, and miaow, and crow, and bray with delight. It was a fine plan! They got ready to carry it out.

First the donkey got up on his hindlegs again and planted his front hooves on the windowsill. Then, very carefully, the dog climbed up on the donkey's back. The cat, with a silent spring, leapt up on to the dog's shoulders. And the cock flew up with the very quietest flutter of his wings and perched on the cat's head.

Now they were ready. At a signal from the donkey, they all began to sing. It was a mixture of braying, and howling, and barking, and miaowing, and purring, and crowing. It made a startling noise. The robbers in the room leapt to their feet, wondering what on earth was happening. Their wicked faces turned pale. And at that moment the donkey pushed open the window and the four musicians leapt into the room. And there was a tremendous sound of braying, and howling, and barking, and miaowing, and purring, and crowing, and crying and shrieking from the robbers.

Well. Even if you're a hardened robber you don't stay in a room at night-time when a strange noise outside the window has been followed by something with wings and

hooves and several tails leaping through the window, braying and howling and barking and miaowing and purring and crowing all at once.

In short, leaving their dinner on the table, the robbers ran away.

The musicians were delighted. "Hurrah!" cried the donkey. "Food! Bones!" cried the dog. "Drink! Milk!" cried the cat. "Comfort! And corn!" cried the cockerel. "Hmm, carrots!" cried the donkey. "I smell fish!" cried the cat.

"Let's eat!" said the donkey.

And eat they did – everything they could find, until they wanted nothing more but a long comfortable night's sleep. So out went the light, and the donkey lay down on a pile of straw, and the dog stretched out on a mat by the back door, and the cat curled up in front of the fire, and the cockerel flew up on the roof and perched there very happily, and they all went to sleep and dreamed of food and music.

BUT . . .

The robbers had not gone far. They were among the trees close to the cottage, watching and listening and plotting and whispering. And when the light went out, and everything became quiet, one of them went to find out what was going on.

He crept through the garden gate, up the garden path, through the front door, and into the room. It was completely dark. He groped for a candle. There was one on the table. He looked round for something to light it with. In the hearth he saw something bright and shining. The dying embers of the fire, he thought. So he bent down and blew to kindle the embers. To his horror the embers sprang at him and scratched his face. For, as you will have guessed, they were really the cat's eyes shining in the dark.

And now the robber crept no more. He ran as hard as he could straight for the back door, and tripped over something. It bit him in the leg, and it barked. Then he ran twice as fast, into the yard, and there something gave him a kick behind, and it brayed. And the robber yelled, and that woke up the cockerel, and he stood there on the roof and shook his feathers and began to crow.

And the robber didn't stop running until he'd reached the rest of the robber band.

"There's a witch sleeping on the hearth," he cried, "and she jumped up and scratched my face! Oh, I wouldn't go back there for worlds! And there's a man with a knife by the door and he stabbed me in the leg! Oh, not for a fortune would I go back! And there's a great monster in the yard, and he beat me with a club! You'll never see me in that cottage again! And on the roof there's a devil, and he stood up and he shouted, 'Robber Doodle, Robber Doodle, shoo!' So I ran away, I can tell you that, I ran away as fast as my feet would take me, and if you've any sense you'll do the same. Run!"

And that's what they did. Off they ran, and they never came back.

As for the four musicians, they never got to Bremen, so we've no idea how well they would have got on with their music. The cottage was so comfortable that they decided to stay there and make it their home. And there was no one to drive them away, or to complain because they couldn't carry sacks of corn, or hunt, or catch mice, and no one threatened to roast them for dinner.

By the way, they do sing sometimes in the long winter evenings, for their own enjoyment. They bray, and bark, and howl, and miaow, and purr, and crow, and it's all very wonderful.

For permission to reproduce copyright material
acknowledgement and thanks are due to the following:

Harper and Row, Publishers, Inc. for "Giacco and His Bean"
from *Picture Tales from the Italian* by Florence Botsford (J. B.
Lippincott) Copyright, 1929, by Florence Botsford; V. H.
Drummond for "The Flying Postman"; Viking/Kestrel for
"Brainbox" from *The Lion at School and Other Stories* by
Philippa Pearce (© Philippa Pearce 1971)) Leila Berg for
"The Lory Who Longed for Honey" from *The Nightingale*
published by O.U.P.; James Clarke and Co. Ltd for "The
Enormous Apple Pie" by Diana Ross; The James Reeves Estate
for "The Cat and the Mouse" (© James Reeves) from *The
Gnome Factory and Other Stories* published by Puffin; Diana
Ross for "Prickety Prackety" from *The Tooter* published by
Faber and Faber Ltd; Pavilion Books Ltd, London for "The
Wonderful Cake-Horse" by Terry Jones from *Fairy Tales*; Faber
and Faber Ltd for "Tim Rabbit" by Alison Uttley from *The
Adventures of No Ordinary Rabbit*; J. M. Dent and Sons Ltd for
"Don't Cut the Lawn!" from *The Downhill Crocodile Whizz and
Other Stories* by Margaret Mahy.

TITLES IN THE SERIES